The Hunger File

John O'Connell

Oak Grove Books

About the author:
John O'Connell is a former student of St Columb's College, Derry, and University College Galway, where he graduated with a B.Comm (Hons.) in 1987. He trained and worked as an accountant in Belfast, before a stress illness interrupted his career. Since leaving accountancy in 1997 he has written several books, *The Hunger File* being the fourth one published. He has previously written *My Name is John...* (1999), concerning his manic-depressive illness, *Love is the Answer: The SDLP, Christianity and the Northern Ireland Conflict* (2002) and *The Calling of Sinead* (2003). He has also written and published the pamphlet *An Irish Velvet Revolution – Achieving a united Ireland through repartition* (February 2004). He resides in Derry city.

First published in September 2004 by Oak Grove Books:
info@oakgrovebooks.fsnet.co.uk

© John O'Connell
All rights reserved.
The moral right of the author has been asserted.

ISBN 0 9537137 3 3

Printed and bound by Antony Rowe Ltd, Eastbourne

All rights reserved. No part of this publication may be reproduced or transmitted in any form or by any means, electronic or mechanical, including photocopy, recording, or any information storage or retrieval system, without permission in writing from the publisher. The book is sold subject to the condition that it shall not, by way of trade or otherwise, be lent, re-sold or otherwise be circulated without the publisher's prior consent in any form of binding or cover other than that in which it is published and without a similar condition including this condition being imposed on the subsequent purchaser.

For the love of the Irish, the jewels in God's crown

Chapter One

It was a desperate way to pass the days of my vacation, but it was the way things were. It was hot, dry and cramped in my temporary home, which the walk-in wardrobe of my apartment had become. I was too afraid to leave the wardrobe for fear that I might be seen and informed on by one of the many republican stooges who lived in the area, and who the IRA would no doubt be telling that I was a fugitive of their kangaroo justice system.

If the IRA caught me I would be dead in minutes. After all, I had seen to it that one of their favourite sons had become the subject of a criminal prosecution and would go to jail for tax avoidance offences at the very least and at most he would probably go to a high security prison that would befit the extent of his involvement with the terrorist organisation.

It was a dreadful scenario, now that I had a chance to see things more clearly. My pride had got me into trouble in a way that I had never thought possible. I was possessed with a desire not to be seen to be weak in the context of the IRA attempting to use me for cover for one of the biggest catches that the Inland Revenue investigation team had ever made in Northern Ireland.

I had stood up to the IRA and I was feeling the utter terror that that entailed. Undoubtedly, I had lost the run of myself. I had picked my enemy unwisely, and I was suffering.

I got off my backside in the wardrobe, and stood among the suits, shirts and coats as they dangled from their hangers. I needed to stretch my legs. Opening the door of the wardrobe slightly, I looked to see if it had got dark yet outside my ground-floor apartment. It was dark.

I opened the door of the wardrobe fully, but very slowly to ensure that I would not be spotted by anyone, and moved on my hands and knees over to the door of the bedroom.

I opened the door of the bedroom, again very slowly, and crawled to the toilet. It was really stinking, as I couldn't flush it for fear that someone would hear that I was home, and I couldn't open a window since someone might notice it outside and realise that I was inside.

I did the bare essentials and cleaned myself, almost instinctually putting my hand on the handle to flush the toilet. I just pulled my hand back at the last instant. I shuddered to think that I might have given myself away for the sake of a good bowel movement.

I was horrified at what I had become in the previous few days since I had finally made my decision to provoke the IRA into killing me by landing their top man in jail.

I was reduced to a nervous wreck, who spent his days hiding in a wardrobe, burping, farting and pissing into empty bottles just to keep myself sane.

I had been on the run for so long then that I could not recall a time that I was not hounded by these "terrorists", as the British called them. But they were more than that to me. They were the carriers of the black plague, a plague so deadly that it was certain that they killed whoever crossed their paths. I had crossed their paths. I had crossed them, simply.

I moved over to my kitchen, again on my hands and knees, switched off the fridge, which I had learned from previous experience sent out such a bright beam of light it was fortunate that I had not already been found by the IRA, and opened the fridge door. I still had some fresh milk, eggs and butter there.

I pulled out a box of Branflakes from a cupboard, and poured them into a bowl, the same bowl I had been using for five days now. I added the milk, and a little sugar, and sat eating on the floor of the kitchen. I was so hungry, my stomach was rumbling like a growling dog.

I ate quickly but quietly as I sat out of sight, hoping that the IRA would not choose this moment to break into my apartment again.

I listened intently to the noises in the flat and outside in the street. I could hear creaks, and squeaks, that I had never noticed in my apartment before this survival nightmare. I had concluded that there were mice underneath my floorboards, and that they were attempting to gnaw and scrape at the underside in order to make a path into my apartment where they must have felt that a ready supply of food was awaiting them.

Outside there was the occasional passer-by, and I was fearful that he or she was in reality a scout for the Provos, and that they were attempting to find me and punish me for the loss of their gangster friend, big Tom.

I shuddered every time I heard footsteps. The path to my door was such that it meant that they were very close by, and would be able to hear any unusual sounds from within, where I was almost trembling at the thought of the door being kicked in again.

As I finished my meal, eating the crunchiest cereal going, I assumed, I sighed in relief. At least no-one would hear me eating now, and that was progress. I put the bowl back in the exact place on my table that it had sat when the Provos had last visited, and I made to crawl back to my hiding place.

As I got there I discussed in my mind the possibility that someone had contacted the newspapers and had warned them that I was to be shot. I was hoping against hope that the press would then declare that I should be spared, and castigate the Provos for being a brutal, psychopathic organisation.

I went further in my mind to recall debates that I had already conducted in my elevated consciousness where I had concluded that the IRA was an evil organisation, just as evil as the British government they were fighting.

I knew they were evil now. I knew it with a certainty that only a man on death row could know. Just as the man who, while existing on death row, could reasonably conclude that the society that had judged him and sentenced him to death was totally unjust, I had come to the conclusion in a heightened sense of awareness that the Provisional IRA was an evil organisation.

They were evil in the sense that they were not good, that they did not value goodness, and that they oppressed people who attempted to be good. They were, in effect, fighting against good people because they believed them to be weak and compliant in the presence of the British.

They were, in short, fighting against good, and promoting evil because evil was a more powerful tool than good in ridding the country of the British. Good was losing out when they were being promoted, and when they were riding high in their military campaign.

Suddenly there was a shuddering noise in the apartment and I jumped slightly. But I quickly realised that it was the oil-fired central heating coming on automatically at the time I had set weeks previously when the winter was at its height. I had meant to cut down on it, but had forgotten to do so, and so had to be contented with my situation in the warmest apartment in the city of Derry.

I crawled into the warmest wardrobe in the city and sat motionless on the floor beneath my clothes. I was terrified again. They would get me soon and I knew it. It was no place to hide, and yet everywhere I had previously hidden they had been able to track me down and find me.

Something told me that it was safer to be at home, in the place they would be least likely to look for me. There was some perverse logic to my thinking in that they had come to the apartment only once and they hadn't searched it for some reason. They probably hadn't expected to find anything.

I had sat in the wardrobe, and listened to their idle chat as the two operatives had moved around my apartment, seemingly there for no particular reason. Yet one admitted to the other that they were there to see if I had left anything for them. They must have been unable to take in the enormity of the action I had taken against their organisation, and felt it possible that it was all a mistake. I smiled at the very thought.

Then, all of a sudden, I heard voices coming through my door again. I crouched up tightly, not daring even to breathe in case anyone had the temerity to enter the bedroom.

But I recognised the voices. For a moment I didn't know who they were, but the voices pleased me.

Then it hit me. It was my mother and my brother. I pushed against the back wall of the wardrobe very fiercely in order to throw myself out of it, through the door and onto the floor of the bedroom. Instinctually, I didn't want my family to know that I had been hiding, and especially not hiding in a wardrobe.

I scampered to my feet, and walked clumsily to the bedroom door.

'Jesus, there he is!' my mother shrieked, as I opened the door and walked to the living room.

'You've been robbed,' my brother said immediately. 'Your front door is wrecked.'

'I know,' I said.

'There's someone in the car who wants to speak with you,' my mother said. I cringed. I thought it was yet another republican, but I tried not to show my anxiety to my mother.

A man walked in. I knew it was a man by his heavy footsteps. I made to face him and I put my hand on a bread knife just in case. But it was the parish priest. He raised his hands into a submissive posture on seeing me.

'It's alright, John,' he said. 'It's all over now.'

'How do you mean?' I asked.

'They've come to myself,' he explained, 'and they've asked that I convey the message to you that it is all over. The threat against your life has been lifted.'

'How?' I wondered.

'I don't know the details,' Fr Doherty said. 'But you're to expect a phone call when it will all be explained.'

'Why?' I wondered.

'They say that they're showing you the respect that you deserve,' he said.

'What?' I wondered.

'It's all over,' he explained. 'Sit yourself down and take a deep breath.'

I sat down and breathed deeply. Something had happened, I thought, and they were backing down. But the relief hit me like a shower of flower petals from heaven. The tension left me and I was happy.

Then the telephone rang.

Chapter Two

The problems began months before. I was a young accountant with a big future if only I learned to keep my head down and my mouth shut. But I hadn't acquired that skill as yet. I was much too wary of the world around me.

I would never miss a trick. I could assess a set of accounts and know whether the punter was playing by the rules or not. Most of them were. Most never needed a tax investigation as the Inland Revenue always knew that their books were reasonably clean and that they would find nothing.

Nearly all our clients skimmed a little off the revenues of their businesses, but only such that they would never get caught. It was an accepted practice to take a little of the petty cash that flowed through their businesses and spend it so that it could never be traced.

Of course, many of our clients were living on low cash drawings from their businesses, which didn't tie in with the prestigious addresses they lived at in the city of Belfast. There was obviously a little bit of mischief going on there, since these families were 'well-to-do', and clearly they would require substantially more money from their businesses to keep them in the standard of life they would be accustomed to.

I knew that, but I didn't ask questions. My boss talked to the clients about those matters and, as it was his signature on the accounts, it never really was a concern of mine.

The new entrants into the firm thought it was great craic seeing how low they could make the profit figure in some of the accounts without actually calculating the client's personal cash drawings as a negative.

Some accounts were like that. Some of them facilitated that approach to finding the answer as to how much the person actually earned in that particular year.

But as you got more experienced you realised that these clients were sometimes 'tearing the backside' out of the whole process, and there was no point in trying to conceal any of their income, when they themselves wouldn't know any different. That was left to the boss who had to get his fee off his client.

There weren't too many tax investigations at that time. They rarely occurred in an experienced accountancy practice with a prestigious reputation. But there was the occasional one, which would annoy the boss, who wouldn't be amused that his accounts weren't being accepted by the Inland Revenue.

My boss, Sean, entered our office one day and told me that a new client we had being working on for a few years had got into trouble with the Inland Revenue. I had never actually worked on the client's books before, so I was feeling particularly pleased that no-one was questioning my work.

A few days later, Sean dumped a heap of bank statements on my desk and told me to get to work on this pile of information as soon as possible. The utmost secrecy was to be exercised in carrying out my duties on this job, which was to summarise the bank statements.

Next day, when I looked at the bank statements, I found out the reason for the secrecy. The amounts involved were substantial, involving tens of thousands of pounds. As I took a closer look over the next few days, I was to come to realise that the amounts involved were in the hundreds of thousands of pounds range.

All I was required to do was to summarise the transactions in the bank statements so as to enable my boss to calculate how much cash had been taken out of the business in each of the offending years, and then to establish how much interest had been earned on the offending cash.

It was not an easy task since the bank statements were of the Money Market variety and had been invested in banks in the tax black spots of the Isle of Man and Jersey.

They had effectively been offshore accounts, despite legally being part of the UK banking system and tax regime. However for many years the practice of the Inland Revenue had been to turn an effective blind eye to the wheeling and dealing in deposits on these island economies.

It was thought that the British government was complicit in this conspiracy by allowing these money centres to bring capital into the UK that would otherwise go to the Caribbean banks.

However, that all seemed to change under Margaret Thatcher's Conservative government. She wanted lower taxes for everyone, especially the rich who had traditionally hidden their capital in Isle of Man and Jersey banks. But the quid pro quo for lower taxation was the closing of the loopholes for tax avoidance and the stricter implementation of the tax laws.

There were rumours that the Inland Revenue had made agreements with the Isle of Man banks, after having discovered that several banks had been involved in illegal transactions to protect the real tax liability of some of their customers.

These customers had been caught out more regularly and their affairs investigated more thoroughly since Margaret Thatcher came to power. It was only a matter of time before a private or corporate customer of an offshore bank was going to get caught out, and leave the entire banking system with egg on its face.

It was rumoured that that had happened, and in order to mitigate its 'debt' to the Inland Revenue, a certain bank had offered to point the taxmen in the direction of several accounts that seemed worth investigating.

Other banks were offered a similar path out of their illegal activities, and it became rumoured that the banks were no longer "safe" on the Isle of Man. In turn Jersey suffered a similar jolt to its reputation as a safe and secure location for large deposits not subject to UK tax.

The problem for the banks was that customers were looking for non-resident status, to exempt them from income tax on bank deposit interest, even when they had addresses within the UK. The banks had complied with the requests for tax exemption, and were caught out by an inquisitive and aggressive Inland Revenue Investigation Branch.

Some bank customers didn't live outside the UK and so their claim for non-resident status was entirely fraudulent.

Our client belonged to this class of culprit. Once the Inland Revenue had got wind of his name and address on the bank statements, they realised that they were onto a sure thing. They were going to pursue him to his grave if the need arose.

As to how they got wind of his details, no-one was sure. He was said to be an extremely careful man, who had obviously seen fit to accumulate vast sums of money in a relatively short period, a seemingly imprudent approach.

It sat in my mind as inexplicable. It was an obvious contradiction. How could this sensible, almost cunning man, who had the sense to move his accountancy work away from his home area in county Derry to another part of the North in case he was caught, or possibly because he had been caught, let himself be caught in the first place?

For the sums of money involved in the deposits, it meant only a flight to the Cayman Islands to ensure that he was never caught. But it was easy to see with the benefit of hindsight.

We had to deal with the situation as it was. He had been caught. It was possibly as a result of some dirty deal that one of the banks he had been using had done to maintain their reputation in the public domain. He had been sacrificed, together with others, to ensure that a bank got out of a very tricky situation with the Inland Revenue, a situation that may have resulted in them losing their ability to trade.

The banks were always shrewd enough to keep their reputations intact. They couldn't trade otherwise. No-one would deal with a bank whose name had been blackened by public scandal, or tarnished by the smear of a tax authority. The Inland Revenue knew that and probably had screwed the sweetest deal out the executives of the bank.

Our client's problems were probably the product of that deal, which had likely been sanctioned in the smoke-filled boardrooms of the bank whose laxity had resulted in the investigation into their affairs taking root in the first place.

It may seem unbelievable to the outsider to the accountancy world that such deals would be the means by which a bank committing a criminal offence could get out of the collapse of its reputation in the public domain. But that was the way it was said to be done in our circles. Putting a bank out of business for doing what all the banks were doing was not good practice.

The Inland Revenue would not risk losing all its debts by forcing a single bank into a corner, possibly forcing it out of business. They would not risk tearing into the bank with investigation teams committed to finding whatever lay in the murky waters there. All they would find might open up a hornets' nest, which might result in the business community getting its back up and the Revenue's powers being curtailed.

They would have less cooperation then from the accountants and lawyers who dealt with the tax affairs of the business fraternity, and that would be the last thing they wanted. There was an uneasy peace between the businessmen and the taxman, which was only breached when someone stood out of line.

Our client had, and whatever way he had come to the attention of the Revenue, he was now subject to their scrutiny. He had to play by a new set of rules, the old set temporarily being set aside by mutual "agreement".

He was to be scrutinized. His affairs were to be put under the microscope of Revenue attention and he was going to have to come clean with them.

Looking at his bank statements, it seemed that he was in a right situation. Some had his name on them, and some had other names on them, perhaps the names of his wife and children, but they all could be traced to addresses in his locality. Not all the addresses were his home address.

It seemed that the Revenue had not provided details of the information that they had found on him. This was intentional, and was a good ploy on the part of the Revenue. It meant that he had to guess what information they had on each particular account. Beyond that, he had to guess which accounts they actually held. He may even have had to guess which particular bank they had got their information in.

The result of this guesswork meant that he might be able to narrow down some of the deposits as being investigated and at risk, and assess others to be free from risk.

But as my work continued it was clear that the amount of money outside the scope of the investigating tax agency's work was not likely to be significant. I couldn't imagine that some small town businessman could have any more money hidden away than the hundreds of thousands of pounds that he had declared to us in the bank statements.

He had probably decided that it was too risky to take a chance on excluding some of the deposits since, if he was caught out, the Revenue might decide to prosecute him in the courts and he might go to jail. So far, with full cooperation, he was on course to stay outside the courtrooms.

That was the practice with the Revenue. If you showed that you were cooperating with their investigation, then you would get off more lightly. If you didn't cooperate, and forced them to show what information they had, and more importantly allow them to prove that you weren't declaring everything, then they would take a dim view of it.

In that scenario, they could insist that you were prosecuted in the courts, and if the court found you guilty of tax fraud, it was likely that you could go to jail. It had happened in many cases, including the case of Ken Dodd and Lester Piggott, that punters, who felt that they were being clever with the Revenue, had gone to jail or been fined punitively for their corruption.

To an outsider it might seem irritating that someone, who like our client had stashed away hundreds of thousands of pounds over a number of years, would be given the option of a private investigation. He should surely have been sent to the courts for prosecution at the earliest opportunity, and ended up serving a lengthy prison sentence.

If he had robbed a bank, and got away with that kind of money, then he would automatically have gone to prison. If the petty thief robs a post office, and gets away with a few thousand pounds, he will almost certainly go to jail.

But if a large businessman defrauds the Inland Revenue out of hundreds of thousands of pounds, then he gets an option of a quiet "gentleman's deal", which might leave him with some of his money intact.

It was a double standard, practised because it was simpler for the Inland Revenue to recuperate their money in this way. It was only money at the end of the day. It was ultimately the businessman's money, which he had decided not to declare to the rest of society so that he wouldn't have as much to pay in tax.

But he may argue that he had earned the money from his businesses. He had put in the effort to allow the surplus profits to be made. He had probably already declared sufficient profit to ensure that his taxes were much higher than average, and he probably felt that that was all he was duty bound to give to the Exchequer.

But the argument was flawed. He had earned more profit because he had used the human and economic resources of the nation more than other people and his tax bill was legitimately higher than average as a consequence. The super-profits that he had hidden away on the Isle of Man were profits made from other people, his customers, who were paying the level of taxes that the government had stipulated for them.

He was only a fool to regard himself as above the law. He wasn't.

He may well have been a fervent Irish Nationalist, and I didn't really know much about him at that stage. He may well have regarded the government as hostile, and thus felt morally obliged not to pay a penny more in taxes than he could get away with.

But that was not evidenced from his desire to hide hundreds of thousands of pounds in illegal accounts in offshore banks. He wasn't giving his money to Ireland; he was taking it from Irish people, albeit Irish people in the UK. He was in effect keeping it for himself, or for his children. He had pursued a selfish agenda.

But it was exciting nonetheless to work on the case. It was exciting because there was so much money involved, and at first I regarded the client as a kind of romantic Irish hero who had attempted to defraud the British Exchequer of a vast amount of money. But he was either a man obsessed with money or a complete fool.

To attempt to get away with such an enormous fraud was foolish in the extreme. He was bound to be caught. No bank was that safe. There would always be whispers, either in his home village where his books were prepared or in the banks themselves on the Isle of Man, where he kept most of the money.

It was such an extensive fraud, involving the client in personally lodging the money in the offshore banks after travelling there on aircraft with piles of cash in his briefcase, that it was almost farcical. It was like something the mafia would do in America.

It was like the actions of a drugs baron, attempting to launder his money through legitimate businesses. However, there was no suggestion that the client had made his money in anything other than a legitimate way. There was no suggestion that he had acted illegally in accumulating the funds.

They were the legitimate profits of his legitimate businesses. He had skimmed the top off his revenues, declaring lower profits than he should have, and furtively hidden the remaining surplus in offshore banks.

But it was more than just skimming. He had literally decapitated the revenues so that what he was declaring to the Inland Revenue was bound to be noticeably different from other businesses of similar size selling similar products.

Perhaps that was the reason why the Inland Revenue investigation team were going easy on him. They should have noticed his fraudulent declarations at a very early stage and thus deterred him from stealing away the rest of the cash. They must have felt some guilt that they let this man literally conceal levels of profit that a blind man would have noticed as fraudulent.

In any case, I felt that there was something wrong with the investigation. I couldn't work it out. Things didn't seem to add up.

But in an accountancy practice, you are expected to accept things that you've been told, and by and large you do. I was actually working with the belief that the big bad Inland Revenue had got its claws onto one of our clients, who had just been putting the money away for a rainy day, or something like that.

Accountants work for the client and at all times we seek to keep his tax liability to a minimum. But we won't do that if someone has been completely irresponsible to the extent that they have effectively brought an investigation upon themselves. Our client had done just that.

The best way out of his predicament, and perhaps the only way out, was for him to declare absolutely everything he had hidden away.

My job was to accurately calculate the amount of tax that would have been due, had the client declared the deposits he made at the correct time. Then I had to calculate the tax due on the interest earned on the undeclared deposit accounts. On top of that the client would have to pay interest on the taxes that he had avoided, and then he would be due penalties.

As in the case of deciding whether he would be prosecuted, the penalties would also be proportionate to the level of cooperation he gave to the investigating officers of the Revenue.

Our client was in a tricky situation, but so far as we were concerned, it seemed that he had provided all the information that was needed to bring the investigation to a close.

Chapter Three

I set all the deposit accounts out on a broad A3 page, and sellotaped another broad page to it so that I could track all the transfers from one account to another. There were twenty-four columns on the two pages combined. This eliminated double counting and facilitated the calculation of the amounts of cash lodged after transfers and interest had been taken into account.

There were reams of pages to go through. Some of the pages were duplicated. That helped since some of them could be discounted. But there were still many left to be summarised and recorded in order to achieve a true reflection of the movement of funds to the offshore accounts.

It was at once tedious and interesting work. It was tedious because it required acute concentration to ensure that no page was unaccounted for, and it was interesting because it involved such large sums of money.

So large were the amounts that I think that my mother would have shot him if she had a gun and she found that this man had wasted so much money by leaving it in a bank. There were entire African countries starving to death while this man sat with several hundred thousand pounds in bank accounts that were never to be used.

More importantly, he didn't need the money. It was surplus to requirements. That's why he had secreted it away in the first place. He was never going to need it.

I think that my mother would have gone berserk at the thought of someone wasting that opportunity to do some good with the money. He could have given it away anonymously if he didn't want to give it to the British Exchequer.

He could have given it to an African charity, who could have saved the lives of tens of thousands of people. Africa had been much in the news as this man had been making his furtive trips across to the Isle of Man. It was the time of Live Aid when Bob Geldof was bursting his gut to get the British and Irish peoples to donate as much of their spare cash as they could for famine relief in Ethiopia.

It was a time when the sight of little children could be seen on our television sets with their bellies swollen for lack of food and with the flies humming around their faces, as if waiting for their carcases to begin to rot. It was a time of immense pain for many people as they witnessed these little children being carried away for burial as the West failed in their human duty to protect the lives of the world's poor.

There were many people, not just my mother, who would have, at those intensely moving moments, taken out their shotguns and blown away that son of a bitch for trying to make himself rich while the world was experiencing starvation.

Perhaps that was why he had come so far to have his accounts dealt with and the investigation carried out. He didn't want to have to face the shame of being seen as so selfish in his home district. He didn't want to be exposed as a hypocrite who went to mass each Sunday, which I assumed he did, and then spent the remainder of his time swindling the rest of his community.

It didn't take that long to get a reasonably accurate picture of his affairs. I worked at it for several days, before I concluded that there was evidence that he was not being totally straight with us. If we noticed this, so would the Inland Revenue. He had to give us more information.

Sean, my boss, agreed and the client was requested to come to a meeting at our office in Belfast. Mr Brennan, our client, agreed to come up.

Tom Brennan arrived at our office at the pre-arranged time on the agreed day. I was not to meet him. Sean was to meet him alone. But I saw him arrive in the car park.

He was driving a very large golden Mercedes Benz, and as he emerged from the car, he looked like a real rich "culchie". He was wearing a beige suit with a beige shirt and a brown tie. He was very presentable, except that his big country face gave the game away. He was not to be messed with. He was tall and slim as if he looked after himself. He looked about fifty years of age if a day, but his clothes looked more suited to a younger man.

Perhaps he was younger than I thought, and the worries of this life, such as his splendid performance on the offshore accounts, had made him look older. But I didn't think so. He seemed cool and collected when he strode into our reception.

He looked like a real J.R. Ewing, in fact. Only the cowboy hat was missing. He was there on business and you could see that he meant business.

When Sean arrived back from the interview room, he seemed pretty happy. The client had more information for us, and it seemed to tie into what we had found to be missing. It seemed that Mr Brennan had come prepared for further questions, and he realised which ones were going to be asked.

Our information looked as if it was complete.

I was astounded when I worked on the last few statements that he had given us. The bank accounts had merged into the one major account, and the balance was well in excess of one million pounds.

How could anyone be so obtuse? So utterly uncaring? So riddled with bravado that he sat with in excess of one million pounds in a bank account while there was need and deprivation in the community he lived in?

He seemed to be an arrogant man, filled with the desires of this world, and forgetful that there were those who would pounce on him eventually when he stuck his neck out too far. Hiding one million pounds away was sticking your neck out too far and saying to the world that you don't give a damn about the rest of them.

We've all felt the need at some time or other to give as little as we could get away with, especially to the Inland Revenue.

But we are rarely so arrogant as to let such monies sit in our bank account. We usually just spend it so that no-one will notice our misdemeanour.

This man didn't care that he would be caught. Perhaps he had an arrangement with the bank officials, and thought that they would never disclose his dishonesty to any third party. Perhaps he had bribed the manager to ensure that his money was safe. He certainly had the wealth to go down that road.

But he had been caught. The arrogant bastard had been caught. I felt that he deserved to get caught if he was sitting with over one million pounds in the bank.

Of course, I wasn't moralising about his hidden money while I was doing the investigative work. It was my job simply to ensure that the money was totalled and the sums done in order to calculate the level of tax due after the money was brought into the realms of the Inland Revenue submissions.

It was for me as a less senior accountant almost a privilege to be involved in such a case, involving as it did well over a million pounds in lost profits. I was delighted that my boss had chosen to engage me in the job. It demonstrated that he had confidence in me.

I was given very little guidance as to what I was supposed to put in the working papers on the file of the firm. It was an unusual job. As I became more experienced, I realised that it was an unusual tax investigation.

The Manchester-based Inland Revenue investigation team didn't seem to want to know very much about the detail of the hidden accounts, and seemed more interested simply in the bottom line as to what they were going to get out of the client.

They seemed to be telling my boss this at the meetings he had with them. He would arrive back to me with estimates of the damage done to date.

'They want £300,000,' Sean told me in the early weeks. He seemed to be guessing, but it seemed like an educated guess.

The estimate then rose from £300,000 to £500,000 to £750,000. The taxman was looking to clean out the client's accounts.

However, when the undisclosed money rose to well over £1,000,000, it seemed that the taxman was looking for at least £1,000,000 to mitigate his loss and our client's fraud. I said to Sean: 'They're looking to take it all.'

I felt that I was right. The taxman was looking to take it all. It was in his interests to take as much as he would be able to get away with. Tom Brennan hadn't a leg to stand on. He had broken the rules in such a way that it was impossible to plead anything but guilty.

Sean didn't disagree with me. He knew that I was right, even if I was not qualified to do anything other than guess. But it was an educated guess. The taxman wanted his tax that, together with interest and penalties, would amount to almost as much as our client had in his illicit offshore bank accounts. It would amount to well in excess of one million pounds.

My friend and former colleague, Peter, was amazed when I hinted to him that I was involved in such a job, involving a million pound tax bill. I was throwing the drinks into me at that stage. Peter was as well.

We were "on the hunt for Red October", as we described our search for a woman in those days of our early twenties. I was probably releasing the stress and tension of my work in the office, which required the utmost professionalism and the highest degree of secrecy.

'What kind of cunt is he?' Peter asked. 'How could he be so stupid as to get caught?'

'Yeah,' I said, 'giving all that money to the British Exchequer, who'll use it to pay to send their soldiers here to harass us.'

'You're a Derry man, John,' Peter said. 'You know what those bastards are capable of. Remember Bloody Sunday. Those boys will be smiling tonight that they've got one of ours paying for their services.'

'I know,' I said.

'That guy should be shot,' Peter mouthed, the drink affecting him. 'If there was any justice in this world, a cunt like that ought to get shot.' Peter knew nothing about the client, and about what connections he might have. I tried to educate him.

'He's the type of boy that would be having others shot,' I said. 'He looks like a real gangster.'

'You've met him?' Peter asked.

'No, I've seen him,' I replied. 'Sean does all the talking.'

'Does that cunt Sean not think he should be shot?' Peter wondered, his hatred for Sean after a dispute he had with his former boss subsiding a little momentarily.

'Sean's getting his fee, a big one at that,' I replied.

'He should be shot too,' Peter gasped, exasperated. 'In fact, shooting is too good for that bastard. He should be hung by the balls till they drop off, and then he should be shot.'

I laughed at Peter's colourful language. It wasn't like him to be so emotional. I realised that he had fallen out with Sean in the recent past, but he seemed out of sorts. Peter had wanted to leave the firm and Sean refused to transfer his contract to another firm nearer to his home, and that rankled.

I decided to cheer Peter up. I got him to move on two women who were standing near us at the bar. We took them out to dance. I was interested in the leaner girl and Peter was keen on the chunkier girl. They were women in their thirties in reality.

We soon got a taxi to my home in south Belfast, where the women came for a cup of coffee and whatever else was on the menu. They were chatty, but not very chatty. I realised that they were on for some fun.

One of them mentioned my bedroom, and so I took my leaner girl, who I think was called Donna, up to have a look. When she lay on the bed, I thought that this was it. She was on for it,

I thought. I lay beside her. We kissed, and I groped her. She didn't mind.

I moved my hand down to her crotch. She didn't mind. I tried to slide her clothes off. She objected. It was going to be one of those nights.

There was plenty of kissing, talking and groping, but no clothes were to be removed. Apparently she was married. I didn't know whether or not she was telling the truth. It seemed consistent with her actions in the bedroom but it wasn't consistent with her actions in coming back to my house.

She told me that if I could make her feel as relaxed as "a big black man" had on the occasion of what was probably her last bit of infidelity, she would be only too delighted to make love. But I couldn't, even if her crotch was soaking wet after our little games.

We went downstairs, where Peter and his babe had remained. They ordered a taxi and went home. Peter told me that he had made love to his girl, but he was filled with laughter as he told me.

'Her fanny shut down,' he laughed. 'She had a muscle spasm, and it closed up half way through. It was awful embarrassing for her. But it was a laugh.'

We burst into laughter. I thought about poor Peter, who had been in bad form all that day, landing himself in such a situation with a chunky big woman, who he hardly knew. It was the last thing he needed. Yet it was better than drinking himself to oblivion at the back of the nightclub.

I arrived late into work next morning, a Friday. I was looking forward to the weekend. The day went slowly, as it always does when you're looking to get out of the place.

The investigation was coming to a close. A few things had to be sorted out, but most of the major areas of work had been completed. I put the file aside to start into again the following week.

I started to work on another job, but my concentration wasn't what it should have been, and I was finding the going slow. I persevered and completed as much of the job as I could.

Timesheets are a feature of the accountancy profession. All professional staff are expected to complete a timesheet, which usually divides the day up into quarter hours so that each period of time is billed to the correct client.

Some jobs required more hours than others. Big jobs can require several hundred hours, whereas the smallest jobs can be completed in a couple of days. My time was charged at thirty pounds per hour.

So big Tom Brennan was getting charged at £30 per hour of my time and it seemed that he was well into the thousands of pounds of accountancy fees at that stage of the investigation.

Sean's time was charged more expensively at over £60 per hour so far as I could discern. So much of big Tom's fee was coming from hours that Sean was putting in. It was strange that Sean never seemed to be working on the job in our office and yet he was clearly charging many hours to the investigation.

I thought that he was overcharging a client in a vulnerable position. I wouldn't have blamed him. The client was a fool to think that he could get away from the prying eyes of the Inland Revenue, and a fool and his money are soon parted. Everyone would want a piece of the action.

However, Sean was more likely to be working on the job at home. He had probably made my job a lot simpler by selecting the information that the Revenue would want, and keeping out anything that would have brought his client more trouble. That way he was probably deserving of all the fee income he charged to the client.

Chapter Four

I went home to Derry for the weekend. I was a typical Derry person working in Belfast, never totally leaving my home city. I felt more comfortable at home, especially at the weekends. I would stay in Belfast occasionally, but only if my money was running low and I didn't want to spend what little I had left going out on the town in my home city.

I had so many friends in Derry still, and as soon as I arrived back, there would be a phone call to tell me what was happening that Friday night and the following Saturday. Drinking was our main occupation.

We would meet up in a pub and drink a few pints. Then we might go to a nightclub. If we were lucky, we would be invited to a party at someone's house.

Brian, my closest friend, was in a right old mood that Friday night. He was downing the pints as if there was no tomorrow. Apparently he had had a row at his work, where one of his subordinates had objected to certain conditions of her employment.

I had heard him talk about it often. She was guilty of insubordination, but he was guilty of bad management. You couldn't tell him that. He seemed to think that he had rights over other people that went beyond the remit of his firm. In fact, he seemed to think that he owned people, lock, stock and barrel.

He would be cursing himself for not being assertive enough, and yet he had no right to be asserting himself in the way that he was suggesting. Ailish, his employee, was fighting her corner, and keeping things the way that they had always been.

He wanted her to be more flexible, without offering her the requisite bribe. Eventually, he did offer it, but she said no, on the basis that she was not going to be bought off over a matter of principle. Her heels had been dug in by the ongoing row, and the lady was not for turning.

It was bad management in a small firm environment. Brian knew it, but wanted to blame Ailish for his troubles. I tried to tell him, and eventually I did tell him directly, but he wouldn't listen to me. I tried to be supportive too, but he interpreted that as meaning that I was coming down on his side.

After a few pints, Brian and I were less preoccupied and more concentrated on the job in hand. The job in hand was to get laid. It was as simple as that. There were girls who were available, and we were seeking them out.

We went to a party that night. I was quite drunk when I arrived at the door with my little bag of tins of beer. It was an awful party. I wanted to go home as soon as I arrived. There were very few women there. It was nearly all men, with their little bags of tins of beer like me.

Eventually, I asked a petite, chunky blond-haired young woman, whom I had always fancied ever since I had seen her around, out for a dance. She was very good-looking and very classy. The music became slow after a while, and I hugged her close to me. I barely knew her name at this stage.

I tried to kiss her, but she moved away. I hugged her even more tightly, ensuring that she didn't go back to her seat. I tried to kiss her again, but she just wanted to talk.

I hugged her more tightly again, and kissed her. She kissed me back. She liked it. We kissed for a few minutes. I was intense and emotional, but it was too dark in the room to see if I was getting anywhere.

I didn't really want to get anywhere with this girl. She was a nice girl from a good family and I wasn't in the mood to breach her innocence. In any case, she seemed as drunk as I was.

I let her go from my "bear hug", and she stood dancing with me for a moment. Then she excused herself, and went to the kitchen.

When next I saw her, she looked at me as if I had grown horns. She was standing in the kitchen, with her male friends, who were all a little more mature than me. Perhaps one of them was her boyfriend, which would have explained her reluctance to kiss me.

I excused myself, and said that I was going.

'Slan,' I said to my dancing partner, the Irish for 'goodbye', and I went on my way. It was a long walk home.

On Saturday night, I went back to the bar where all my friends were drinking.

Kieran, a psychologist friend, was in good form. We got talking about scandals, and I decided to mention to him about the tax fraudster who had been caught by the Inland Revenue for well over a million pounds.

'What motivates someone like him?' I asked the psychologist, who was also a college lecturer.

'Money,' Kieran said.

'There must be more to it than that,' I said.

'Insecurity,' the psychologist replied. 'He had the opportunity and he had the obsession. He may even create the opportunity. But insecurity is at the heart of his troubles.'

'He didn't seem like an insecure man to me,' I said.

'Well,' Kieran said, 'he has to be. What you saw was a façade, but if you take away his obsession, he will crumble.'

'Why?' I wondered.

'He's the kind of person that builds himself up to be something he's not,' Kieran said. 'He probably goes to church, and gives little sums to charity, so as to make himself out to be a generous and community-oriented person. But in reality he wants nothing to do with the community. He only wants everyone to look up to him.'

'But I've heard that he's heavily involved in his local GAA club,' I said. 'Surely he has a passion for the community?'

'No,' Kieran smiled, 'he's probably the treasurer, who has access to the club's finances.'

Kieran's words were interesting to me in a strange way. It seemed that my friend had got this tax fraudster totally wrong. He was a senior official of a GAA club, and I knew from my own experiences with the GAA as a player that the organisation expected one hundred per cent from everyone if they got involved. It was not the place to hide if you were just looking for street credibility.

However, Kieran was usually pretty accurate in his analysis of anyone we had talked about before. Some things just didn't seem to add up.

There was this thing that Kieran had said about the man crumbling if he lost his obsession. Tom Brennan was not crumbling. He was in difficulties, even extreme difficulties, but he seemed to be handling it in a very professional and calm manner. He was certainly not worried about losing all his money, in the sense that he was losing everything that made him what he was in his own eyes.

It crossed my mind that maybe he had more money hidden away, and thus he wasn't all that worried that the Revenue were getting their hands on this "tranche".

I didn't want to go into it any further with Kieran. I decided that it was best that I kept any more details to myself, in case I turned out to be right.

I also decided that I would travel down to the towns in county Derry, where this money had been earned. Perhaps Tom Brennan's businesses were larger than we thought, and perhaps we should be looking out for more hidden investments.

If Kieran was right, then this man could have been risking his freedom by entertaining the thought of outsmarting the Revenue. He could go to jail and there would be a hell of a lot of egg on our faces if we hadn't protected him sufficiently.

What kind of nutter was he? Was he not aware that you couldn't play with the Inland Revenue investigation branch? They'd crucify him if they caught him out.

I needed to see his shops.

Next morning, after mass, I visited my parents for breakfast and told them that I was travelling up to Belfast early because I had some work to do.

The traffic was quiet on the road to Belfast, as I expected on this Sunday afternoon. I turned off the road as I came near Magherafelt, a small town just off the main road from Derry to Belfast.

I drove into the centre of the town. It was eerily quiet since most of the shops were closed. I looked around for Brennan's Autoparts.

Strangely, when I found it, it was smaller than I thought it would be. In fact, it was much smaller than it needed to be. It was closed, but perhaps it had very expensive stock from which to generate profits that I was not able to see. Yet who would it sell this expensive stock to? Cars were no more expensive around this county Derry town than elsewhere. He should only have been making small profit margins.

It was baffling. His shop needed to be much bigger if it was to be making profits so large that he could afford to hide away hundreds of thousands of pounds in one year. If my psychologist friend, Kieran, was right, then he needed to have other money, which meant that he was slating away much more than he was caught for.

For that to be the case, his Autoparts shop needed to be the size of a supermarket, and not the size of a couple of large houses joined together as was the case in Magherafelt.

I needed to go to Coleraine to see his other shop. It had to be much bigger than the Magherafelt shop. In fact, it had to be absolutely massive for Kieran to be right. Coleraine was out of my way, but I decided that this matter was such a puzzle that it was well worth my while to take a look at this other shop and perhaps get to the bottom of the mystery.

Three quarters of an hour later I arrived in Coleraine. I wasn't sure exactly where I was to find Tom Brennan's shop, but as it turned out, I happened to come across it by chance.

I was shocked by what I saw. It was even smaller than the Magherafelt shop. It was big as businesses went in the county Derry town, but it was much smaller than would have been needed for me to be able to conclude that Kieran was right in his opinion that Tom Brennan would crumble, when Tom Brennan wasn't crumbling.

In my opinion, Tom Brennan had no other money, and yet he wasn't crumbling. He would have found it extremely difficult to take the money he had already taken from the businesses, without absolutely "tearing the arse" out of the situation.

Some things just didn't add up. I had to talk to my boss, Sean. He may not have even seen these businesses, and he may not be aware that we needed further explanations from our client as to the nature of these deposits arriving on the Isle of Man and Jersey.

Tom Brennan had to be up to something. It would have been impossible to take any more than forty or fifty thousand pounds per year out of those businesses without someone noticing straight away. There had to be another explanation for the arrival of amounts in the region of £500,000 in any one year into accounts in the offshore banks.

The client was not being straight with us. It kept coming back to the client. But we were his accountants, and we couldn't expose him to such a risk of being found out and prosecuted by the Revenue. If caught, he would go to jail for a very long time.

On Monday morning I asked Sean about the client, being coy about the fact that I had seen the shops. I didn't want him thinking that I was going behind his back. That would imply that I didn't trust my boss in some way.

'He didn't declare an entire trade,' Sean said. 'He thought he would get away with it, but obviously the Revenue got wind of the money.'

'What kind of trade?' I asked.

'Exhausts,' Sean said. 'He kept them out of his accounts. He thought the shops were far enough away from the tax office that the Revenue would never know that he sold exhausts. That way he could keep all the profit to himself.'

'But, Sean,' I said.

'What?'

'He would need to be selling a lot of exhausts in any one year,' I replied.

'How do you mean, John?' Sean asked in a coy fashion. Sean had a habit of pleading ignorance when he knew that you were on to something.

'Five hundred thousand pounds worth of exhausts,' I pointed out, 'would require sales of over a million. He's not that big.' As soon as I said it, I knew Sean would be on to me.

'You've seen the shops?' he asked.

'Yeah,' I admitted, 'I drove past them. I wanted to know if he was hiding money from us. You see, he should be suffering at the moment, but big Tom Brennan doesn't seem to give a damn. I thought he might be holding out on us.'

'Aw,' Sean muttered, 'he gives a damn alright.'

'But he should be devastated,' I said. 'And yet he's striding in here in his Sunday best as if it was just like giving over his weekly offering to the Church. He should be shrivelled up and grey-haired.'

'People suffer in different ways,' Sean said.

'So how to hell does he hide a million pounds worth of sales of exhausts in 1983?' I wondered. I had that look about me that demanded to know the answer.

'I suppose he sourced them over the border or in Europe,' Sean explained. 'He could hide the invoices then, and keep all his cash sales out of the accounts.'

I wasn't convinced, but it was a good explanation. Tom Brennan was a shrewd man and he could get away with a lot of things if he really tried. If there's a will there's way. There certainly was a will, and he had obviously found a way.

But the level of sales still bothered me. It was far too high. Tom Brennan had been totally careless if he decided to try to defraud the Revenue out of that amount of money in a single year. It was far more than careless. It was even more than reckless. It amounted to a level of bravado that made me feel that there was a certain justice to him being caught.

I worked on the job for the remainder of that day. By the end of the day, the profits of his illicit trade in exhausts were summarised neatly on Tom Brennan's file. In 1981, he had taken over £307,132 out of his business and lodged it in an offshore account.

In 1982, Brennan had taken £523,869 out of the business. In 1983, he had taken £354,581 out. In 1984, he had taken £162,090. And in 1985, he had taken £102,354 out of his exhaust profits.

After that he had taken just peanuts out of his business, but the interest earned on the deposits were so significant that he had accumulated around £1,800,000 in deposits by the time we began working on his investigation in late 1990.

'Almost two million,' I sighed. 'What I could do with two million pounds!'

But the Revenue were already looking for most of it. In fact, they were after it all. They would want to teach him a lesson.

Chapter Five

For days I grappled with this appalling anomaly. It couldn't be right, I thought, that this client could simply sell exhausts at that rate.

'He must have sold them to half of Northern Ireland's motorists,' I told Sean.

Sean was perplexed too. Or at least he seemed perplexed on the surface. Perhaps underneath his confused exterior was a man who knew exactly how the money had been generated. Perhaps, he knew that there was a separate shop in another town that the Revenue were not aware of even now, and this shop had been so successful that it had been a real money-spinner.

However, if that was the case, why was there a peak in the cash generated in 1982 and an almost complete disappearance of the illicit funds in the years after 1985? Brennan would have had to be consistent, surely, if he was to avoid being caught.

Sure, the profits declared on his income tax returns rose in those latter years after 1985 so that he was showing significant income by the time of the investigation, but there seemed more to it than that. There was simply no way that he could have generated £500,000 pounds in any one year from trading in exhausts.

Perhaps Sean's real confusion related to getting himself out of the mess he was in. His client was clearly not being straight with him. Perhaps Sean was not being totally straight with me. Perhaps he wanted me to invent a credible reason for his client having such large sums of money on hand in the early 1980's.

He hadn't asked me and I wasn't volunteering. Perhaps he was just lamenting the fact that he had actually given the client the suggestion of using the exhausts as an excuse, and it had, on reflection, turned out to be totally incredible.

Tom Brennan needed a credible plan to get himself out of going to jail. There was little doubt about that. If he went into a meeting with the Inland Revenue special investigation team with his excuse, and they said that they had been to his shops, Tom Brennan would be going to jail for non-cooperation. There was no doubt about that.

On the other hand, if they had all the money in their coffers, then the Revenue might be happy enough with the investigation and not pursue it any further. They might not even make a visit to the shops for fear that they would find more "hornets' nests". They might simply accept that our client had learned his lesson after losing over a million pounds, and not pursue it any further.

It was a long shot, but that seemed to be what Sean was hoping for. He was hoping to tell the Revenue nothing, and get them offside as soon as possible. It was called "the mushroom strategy": keep the Revenue in the dark and fill them full of bullshit.

But the source of the cash troubled me. It was at the back of my mind, niggling and confusing me, for days.

Then something struck me. As the array of cash lodged in the offshore banks sat in front of me one lunch hour, I noticed that the cash was clumped around the early years of the 1980's.

'Fuck,' I said quietly. 'It's hunger-strike money.' I was aghast. It seemed impossible and yet it seemed perfectly appropriate to the circumstance and the attitude of our client.

The hunger strikes of 1981, led by Bobby Sands, elected while on hunger strike as MP for Fermanagh and South Tyrone, had generated great interest in Ireland, Britain, and America. It was said that the IRA had received millions of pounds in cash donations in America especially, and that this money was sent back to Ireland to fight the war with the British.

Even the British miners, who had been defeated after a major strike in 1983 by Margaret Thatcher, the British prime minister who had allowed the hunger strikers to die, had sent large donations to the IRA.

I began to feel hot around the collar as I looked at the sheet of undeclared profits in front of me. The pattern of lodgements could certainly be explained in the circumstances of it being illegal money destined for the IRA.

If the money had been collected in New York, Boston, Philadelphia, and other American cities, and transferred back to Ireland at that time, then the pattern of lodgements would begin in 1981 as it did, and peak in 1982 as the first full year of lodgements, and then decline afterwards. That was exactly what had happened.

I couldn't believe what I had discovered. I had discovered IRA money.

'Jesus Christ!' I exclaimed. 'This is mob money!'

After fobbing off my colleague, Packie, who wanted to know what I meant, I continued to sweat under the collar.

I thought about my predicament for a moment. I was sitting in an office with a client's file in front of me, and it seemed from the information presented to me that the client was a front for the mob.

It is not readily understood outside Northern Ireland, and often not even in areas inside the state, that the IRA is a complex organisation. It is not simply a conglomeration of thugs and murderers who would be readily identifiable on any identity parade.

Sure, they have their thugs and bullies, who they use to exercise control over areas of Belfast, Derry and south Armagh. But the organisation is much more complex than that. It consists of well-heeled businessmen and lawyers and teachers and accountants and just about every type of middleclass person as well.

On the surface it may seem that these businessmen simply do favours for the IRA for which they get favours in return. That may in fact often be the case.

But there was a small core of middleclass people in the hierarchy of the IRA, who controlled such activities as finance and intelligence. Their job was to recruit as many intelligence agents as they could in order to keep the information flowing to the army operatives.

Surely the British intelligence agencies would have known about that, and it would be common knowledge in the Catholic community that the IRA operated in this way? But no, it wasn't in the interests of British intelligence to expose their knowledge of the IRA since this would have motivated more young people to join the even more glamorous IRA, and it would have inflamed the unionists into a violent backlash. It was better to say nothing.

I knew all about the intelligence corps of the IRA. I was almost recruited to it at one stage. I was sitting in the back of a small car with an older accountant in the front waiting to be taken to a Gaelic football match, where I was to play as a centre forward in my local team, when I was approached by a senior figure in the club management.

'What are you like at remembering number plates?' he asked innocently enough as he sat in the passenger seat and leaned over to me.

'Not great,' I said.

'But you're good with numbers?' he said. He was a teacher at my former grammar school, and he was aware that I had a grade 'A' in A'level maths. But his knowledge of my maths score unnerved me and made me suspect that there was something more to the conversation.

'Yeah,' I said dryly, 'but not number plates.'

'Think about it,' he said as he turned around.

'I have,' I muttered.

I was aware that the teacher held strong republican views, and that his chat was not idle. The remembering of number plates was a basic task of intelligence operatives in the IRA. Sometimes they would wait outside police stations and take a mental note of the registration numbers of cars that enter and leave.

At other times they would follow cars that had left the police stations to their homes in what were regarded as safe areas. The information would be passed on to the IRA unit responsible for that area and the police officer would be attacked and possibly killed.

The intelligence operatives were an essential part of IRA activity, and good intelligence made the IRA very successful at times in hitting their targets. These intelligence officers were highly intelligent and highly motivated.

It was, however, a low risk occupation as very few intelligence operatives were ever caught by the security forces. It was the kind of mysterious and romantic occupation that would have interested me had it not been for the presence of a slightly older accountant in the driver's seat.

I simply did not believe that he would be involved in the IRA to the extent that he would have been trusted with hearing such a conversation. It seemed totally out of character. But it takes all sorts.

So I was aware of the middleclass involvement in the IRA. I was aware that many of these people would have connections in the religious world since my former school was run by the Catholic Church. They were possibly members of the Knights of Columbanus, an elite society of Roman Catholic lay people who ostensibly did charity work.

But the Knights also had a reputation for breaking the rules on occasions by involving themselves in disputes that had effected members of their society, and thus there was a Masonic scent about them. It wouldn't take a fully-fledged conspiracy theorist to work out that some members would see the Northern Ireland conflict as an opportunity to fight the old war with Protestantism.

Nonetheless, my mind was open to the odd conspiracy theory, and I figured that the real size of the IRA was enormous since it involved just about every echelon of society.

What was I to do now that I had almost certainly uncovered a massive amount of IRA cash, and was probably working on a case which might lose the IRA well over a million pounds?

I had to talk to Sean. But Sean could be involved too. Why else would big Tom Brennan, the possible godfather of godfathers of the IRA, come to him? He had to be involved in some way. He had at least to be trusted.

I didn't know what Sean's politics were. I assumed that he was an SDLP supporter.

Were there elite supporters of the SDLP in the IRA, I wondered, who had perhaps evolved from a time in the 1970's when Sinn Fein were not in electoral politics? Had they supported the SDLP position then, and regarded Sinn Fein's entry, as a very working-class party, with disdain? Who did the IRA really support?

The 1987 Enniskillen bombing came to mind. It had been set off in an area where the emerging Sinn Fein party had decimated the SDLP, and the bombing had reversed the fortunes of the SDLP and decimated Sinn Fein. Was the Enniskillen bombing deliberately designed to damage Sinn Fein? Was it a deliberate attempt to destroy Sinn Fein's electoral hopes?

Was the IRA really controlled by members of the Knights of Columbanus, who despised Sinn Fein's almost communistic tone and their lack of faith in God?

There were all sorts of questions flashing through my mind. Did the intelligence section of the IRA, made up of eager young professionals, actually have any contact with the soldiers, who fought in the IRA's active service units? The answer was probably 'no'.

I had possibly discovered a secret of the IRA. Elements were supportive of the SDLP position while, at the same time, the organisation had to keep sweet the cannon fodder in the active service units, who had strong links with Sinn Fein.

But was Sean one of those secret IRA intelligence officers, or was he just a sympathiser? He could have been either. I wasn't sure, as he was secretive about his political views. He had never discussed them with me.

Nonetheless, he was a businessman, and a fairly rightwing one at that. Businessmen tended to like to have armies around when the going got tough since it gave them an opportunity to struggle for their markets.

Unionist businessmen had used the UVF in the early part of the last century to bring Northern Ireland into existence in order to protect their markets in Britain. Why wouldn't Catholic businessmen do likewise when they had the opportunity?

Wars tend to make businessmen feel powerless if they had no part in any army. In a sense, wars brought the worst out in businessmen. They would ingratiate themselves with the army of occupation, of whatever kind, in order to maintain the profitability of their business.

In many areas of the North of Ireland, the IRA was the stronger army on the ground, and it may have been tempting for many businessmen to help out with donations of cash and jobs for the boys. They were then part of the war effort, and they will have believed that it was a just war.

Many businessmen will have believed that, especially after Bloody Sunday in Derry in 1972, when fourteen innocent Catholic men were shot dead, it was the entirely appropriate that the Catholic community should go to war.

Perhaps even members of the SDLP, including elected representatives, had decided that it was appropriate to go to war in whatever way they could, and that was when the membership of the IRA really exploded.

At that time, of course, Sinn Fein was just a publicity arm of the IRA, and the SDLP would then have assumed the role of politicians for the entire Catholic community. There must have been some who believed that the British had to be taken on after Bloody Sunday.

The SDLP deputy-leader of that time, John Hume even suggested that the Irish government begin recruiting in the North after Bloody Sunday, where he suggested they would find 50,000 young men ready to fight in its army. But that was a long way from supporting the IRA.

I approached Sean as soon as I saw him enter his office. I gave him a chance to settle at first, then bombarded him.

'Look at this money coming into those accounts,' I told him as I held Tom Brennan's summary sheets up for him to see.

'What John?' he asked.

'Look at the dates,' I said, pointing to the date column of the sheet.

'What?' Sean seemed baffled.

'1981, 1982, and 1983,' I said. 'That's when most of the cash was lodged.'

'What does that mean?' Sean wondered.

'Hunger strikes, Sean,' I said with heavy emphasis on my words. 'It's hunger strike money.'

'Tom Brennan's not like that, John,' Sean said dismissively.

'Oh, I know, Sean,' I said, nodding my head in agreement. I had made my point. It was for Sean to assess what kind of risk we were in personally or the firm was in collectively as a result of this piece of information.

I had agreed with Sean as I saw no way of pointing it out to him. Either he suspected it or he didn't. Sean was no fool. He could smell a rat at a hundred paces. There was no point trying to argue with him that his client was an IRA godfather if he was prepared to dismiss instantaneously what I was showing him.

It seemed as if Sean was prepared for the question. It seemed that he dismissed it too quickly. It was a reasonable possibility as Sean hardly knew the client, and yet Sean dismissed it as if it was matter of him being an Arsenal Football Club supporter, or something as frivolous as that.

Tom Brennan was involved heavily in the GAA. That meant he had republican ideals, violent or non-violent. He was a wealthy businessman who could not demonstrate to a reasonable mind how he had come to be in possession of almost two million pounds. It was right for us to suspect him.

Chapter Six

Sean's dismissal of my suspicions was a blow to my confidence in some ways. I felt that he should have let me know what his thinking was. It was too obvious that all was not right with our client's explanations for Sean to make me feel as if I was paranoid.

I wasn't in the slightest bit paranoid and yet Sean refused to acknowledge what I had said to him. He shrugged it off on occasions with a cheap joke.

'Big Tom, an IRA man,' he laughed as if to use his advantage of knowing the client to dismiss my "irrational" conclusion.

'Stranger things have happened,' I said. 'We need to be careful.'

'But that idiot is no IRA man,' Sean said.

Tom Brennan was some idiot. He drove a £60,000 car, a really fancy one that stood out like a sore thumb on the roads. He walked like a man who meant business, striding across the firm's car park as if he owned the place. He seemed like the kind of man who would have spat on you if he saw you in the gutter, and then told everyone that you had asked for a drink, and that he was just obliging.

He was a tough guy. He hadn't got where he was then without a strong will and a dogged determination to get what he wanted in life. He was a self-made man, who had demonstrated considerable courage in dealing with the Inland Revenue.

Even if it wasn't his money to lose, he could go to jail for non-cooperation. That was the approach he was taking so far as I was concerned. His explanations were almost a joke. He may have felt that if it came to the crunch, he could pull the IRA out of the bag and nail the tax inspector with threats that he would be shot if he tried to get a conviction.

For all I knew, that approach had possibly already been made to the Inland Revenue inspector, and all his subsequent investigations were a sham to cover the fact that he was going to go leniently on big Tom. Perhaps that was why big Tom was so calm. But that wasn't credible since the Revenue were going to take well over one million pounds from our client in the investigation.

Another reason I thought of for his calmness was that big Tom was putting on a brave face in line with his position as an integral part of the IRA organisation. He was effectively saying that he would serve the time, or "the bird", if need be, as so many of his comrades had done over the course of the long war with Britain.

It probably wouldn't pay him to act like a wimp. If he was seen to let the side down then he might have been disregarded in true IRA fashion, by laying him out on the side of a south Armagh road with a hood over his head and a few bullets between his ears.

That was not, however, how the IRA acted with businessmen, especially not ones who had been loyal to them for several years. Big Tom, if he showed any weakness, would possibly be signed into a mental institution for his own safety, and the remainder of his representatives would conduct the investigation on his behalf.

Big Tom had no intention of going down that road, so whatever he was going to do, he would not be showing any display of weakness.

Perhaps Sean was right then; perhaps he was quivering under the pressure, a real idiot, but was afraid to show it in public. Perhaps he had explained that to Sean and Sean was protecting him out of decency.

But I knew Sean well enough to be curious about his political views. He was a cunning man in business, whose shrewdness seemed to know no bounds. He was from a rural area of county Tyrone where he had been raised on a farm.

He had been involved with big business in the Republic in his career, which could have ignited republican tendencies.

When he came to Belfast his clients were primarily based in west Belfast, even though he had a city centre office. He had lived in north Belfast, and he was a Church-going good citizen, who had all the hallmarks of membership of the Knights of Columbanus.

He was probably a typical Knight, in that he was only involved in their affairs on the periphery, but if he was involved, then he felt it important enough to be involved.

Perhaps he wasn't involved at all, and big Tom Brennan was the only real Knight in our midst. Sean may only have been a trusted insider, who had sufficient knowledge of Inland Revenue investigations to enable him to do a good job for his client as well as for the IRA.

Sean would have been trusted because he came from a republican area outside Belfast, and like myself, he may have expressed strong sympathy for the plight of west Belfast's Catholic population. In that sense, his concerns for his fellow citizens may have been interpreted as an indication that he was prepared to play ball.

At the very least, it would have been interpreted as meaning that he would be unwilling to shop his client to the RUC or British army intelligence.

I was slightly baffled by the whole scenario. Here I was, doing a job to the best of my ability, and being put in the frontline in the battle between the British Crown and the IRA. There was no doubt about that bit. The IRA were being challenged by the British government's tax collecting authority. They were lucky not to be dealing directly with the police or British army intelligence.

I wondered if I was in any danger. Was there a chance that this investigation could become nasty and the police called in to make a prosecution? Even if the police were only brought in to investigate tax fraud, it wouldn't take a Sherlock Holmes - with a bit of knowledge of big Tom Brennan's businesses - two minutes to work out that our client was lying.

If he stuck to his story, Tom Brennan would be in Castlereagh holding centre speaking to Special Branch investigators before he could say, "it was the exhausts!"

Clearly it wasn't the exhausts. They simply could not have produced the level of profits that he was now declaring. There had to be another source. The only explanation that I could see, or that a cop would see, would be that he was laundering money on behalf of the IRA.

The dates gave it away. The money started to come in during and after the hunger strikes, peaking in the immediate aftermath of those strikes, and falling away in subsequent years. It clearly indicated that big Tom Brennan had been helping out, perhaps as an extra source to deal with the overflow of cash that probably "afflicted" the IRA in those years.

Clearly he had only been helping out since the time of the 1981 hunger strikes, and not before, or else he would have had other accounts to deal with. We were talking specifically about a flow of cash that came the IRA's way after the deaths of Bobby Sands and his comrades, and which related to the massive public sympathy across the world at their treatment by Margaret Thatcher.

But the fact still remained that I was at risk of being implicated in this investigation if it was ever carried out by the police. Even a junior accountant with no experience would have smelt a rat if he saw the large sums of money that were supposed to be coming from an illicit trade in exhausts.

No business in Northern Ireland, even in the cities of Derry and Belfast, could make £500,000 a year from their exhaust trade. The likelihood of two medium size businesses in two fairly average sized towns making that kind of money would be so remote that it was laughable.

Nonetheless, the joke was on me. I was the one at risk if the RUC raided our office. I had compiled the figures and the ever-observant police officers of Special Branch would say that I could not have failed to notice the irregularities.

I would be down in Castlereagh holding centre myself then. Sean and big Tom would be in the cells next to mine, and we would all be arguing our innocence. I could easily be convicted on the basis that I was complicit in the conspiracy even if there was no evidence against me.

Stranger things have happened in Castlereagh. Innocent men have spent years in prison on the basis of false confessions attained there. Even guilty men had been convicted of the wrong crimes after a few days in Castlereagh. I was in a tricky situation.

My friend Brian, from Derry, called at my digs in Belfast that Thursday night and we went out on the town. I needed to relax and get things into perspective. It was a tricky situation and one that could lead to my downfall. Brian was shocked when he heard an outline of the problem.

'Fucking IRA money!' he exclaimed in a whisper. 'You want to be careful there.'

'I'm trying to be,' I said.

'Resign,' he urged me. 'There's plenty of jobs for accountants in Derry.'

'I couldn't leave the job in the hands of some junior trainee accountant,' I said. 'They would be mauled. I need to resolve the matter, not make it worse.'

'It's not your problem,' Brian said.

'It is,' I said.

'How?'

'It's been my problem from the moment that those summary accounts were prepared,' I replied. 'I'm knee-deep in shit, and even if I leave now, the cops would never believe that I was right just to keep my mouth shut.'

'You know what I think you should do,' Brian said quietly, lowering his voice as if he was surrounded by cop informers in the busy nightclub. 'I think that you should go to the cops now.'

'What!' I exclaimed. 'Are you fucking crazy?'

'Why not?'

'Because I would be on the run for the rest of my life,' I replied.

'You don't have to tell anyone that you informed,' Brian said. 'Your client would just go to jail on the evidence on your file. You wouldn't have to be a witness.'

'It's a big risk,' I said. 'You know the cops. Once they have you in a compromising position, they screw you for the rest of your life.'

'Think about it,' Brian said.

In actual fact it was a tempting thought. I could even use the confidential telephone line to lead the cops to their arrests without getting involved myself, and even if they arrested me, I could always get out of it by saying that I was the informant who had contacted them in the first place.

But the IRA were no fools. They would source it to me eventually, and see to it that I never did it again.

In any case I had no loyalty to the RUC. They were a brutal police force who had demonstrated their contempt for my community on many occasions. They were 90% Protestant in a state where around 40% of the populace was Catholic. They had also violated so many human rights that I could understand why people wanted to kill them.

I wasn't particularly pacifistic by nature, and if I thought that the Northern Ireland problem could be resolved by fighting the RUC and the British army, then I would have been in there too. But I was a strong supporter of the SDLP, whose rationale was to resolve the conflict through dialogue.

Two women approached us in the nightclub and Brian beckoned me to make a move.

I asked one of the girls out to dance while Brian stood chatting to the other one. Bernie was my girl's name. I danced with Bernie for a few songs. We embraced when a slow set came on, and eventually we kissed. I got dug into her on the dance floor. She was a fantastic kisser.

Her large breasts pushed into me and looking down her cleavage made me feel very horny. Bernie was tall, slim, with big breasts and a very curvy figure. She was well-dressed in a short, summery dress that accentuated her curves. She had beautiful blond hair, wavy and sexy. She was the kind of girl who would turn you on just by looking at her.

By the time I came off the dance floor I had practically got an erection. Bernie knew this and was smiling away at me. When we got back to Brian and her friend, Bernie whispered something in her friend's ear while she sat on a seat near the bar. Her friend's eye level was just adjacent to my crotch, and whatever Bernie said to her, she immediately laughed and grabbed me by the balls.

'Hey! Big balls!' she shouted.

I moved back clumsily and instinctually out of embarrassment, and fell over a couple who were sitting kissing on the seats next to us. It was very dark, and no-one noticed what Bernie's friend was pointing out. I sat uncomfortably on the edge of a seat until my embarrassment had reduced in size and the fuss was over.

Brian and I offered Bernie and her friend a lift home, and we got into the car outside the nightclub.

Bernie came home with me, and her friend took Brian home.

Bernie, or Bernadette, as she sometimes liked to be known, was a fun girl. She slept with me on that first night, but wouldn't have sex. I lay awake the whole night, trying to get her to change her mind, and unable to relax with such a beautiful pair of breasts next to me in the bed.

They were so beautiful, firm and full. She was just blossoming as a young woman. She was the most attractive young woman that I had ever bedded.

Eventually in the morning, I remembered that I had a condom in my wallet, and I suggested to Bernie that it would do no harm to have sex, "just the once".

Surprisingly she agreed. The sex lasted about thirty seconds, so horned up was I by just lying next to her.

'Jesus,' Bernie laughed, 'if I had known it would only take that long, then I would have let you go ahead last night.'

'It would have taken a lot longer last night,' I protested.

Bernie was a fine filly. She was a Belfast girl from a working-class background in west Belfast.

She would have been a fine catch were it not for her very strong working-class accent, which sounded a bit naive. She was an innocent kind of character in most things, but when it came to sex she seemed very advanced.

She told me that she had been in a relationship with a bar manager for four years, despite not being all that much younger than me, and that she had lived with him. That explained her sexual proficiency.

Chapter Seven

Strange things began to happen after I met Bernie. It was a time when I was still figuring out how I should handle my delicate situation in the office.

Should I simply hold my nerve and see the investigation through, as Sean was doing, or should I act to ensure that I was safe and not at risk of being prosecuted as an IRA stooge? It was a difficult question.

The IRA was a strange organisation. To me, it was a politically motivated murdering machine made up of men who would cut your throat if they thought that you had crossed them. They had murdered many people in the North of Ireland and beyond.

I had a strange loyalty to them as a young boy. They were kind of heroes to all the young boys in the district because we thought that they were fighting against the evil British army who had no right to be in our district, or in any part of our city.

There was a Catholic majority in Derry. That meant that the British were not welcome, and indeed, when we saw them on our streets, we saw them as an alien army trying to repress our people.

But we saw the human side to the soldiers as well. They would talk to us and show us their guns, and take out the rounds of ammunition so that we could know just how great these men were. They were so powerful with their guns and their armoured personnel carriers, which we called "pigs" because they looked like pigs.

We rarely saw IRA men on our streets. They only ever showed themselves in the ghettos, where the writ of the British army was under threat. So we had no way of knowing what IRA men were really like.

We knew that they were tough and that they could kill soldiers by shooting at them or by bombing them, but we didn't know what they were really like.

As we got older and the conflict was still raging, we began to challenge our childhood instincts, and assess the IRA in a more sceptical way.

The IRA claimed to be fighting for Ireland, but they had done so much damage to the Irish people that their campaign was not a simple matter of getting the British army out of the country.

There were no jobs for us in Derry, and yet the IRA had shot an American industrialist dead, and bombed many factories and businesses out of existence. We had to ask whether the IRA were interested in a settlement of the problem, or whether they were interested in starving the Catholic community of jobs to make them more likely to support them.

It was a cynical plan if it were true, but the IRA had proven their cynical credentials on occasions, and there was no doubt in my mind that they were capable of going down that path.

They had ruthlessly killed Catholics as well as Protestants during the course of the conflict. Many of their own members, who had been found to have cooperated with the British security forces, were found along the roads of south Armagh with hoods over their heads, having been shot to death for their disloyalty.

There was no simple answer in relation to the IRA. The whole Northern Ireland conflict was such a mess of contradictions and paradoxes that no-one could really take a clear view of any part of it. For me, it came back to the position that all violence was wrong, no matter who was carrying it out. That was the only road to peace.

I was a supporter of Nobel Peace Prize winner John Hume and his party, the SDLP. I didn't like violence, and I had concluded over time that it would not help to resolve the conflict.

But there were others, who existed on the periphery of the violent paramilitary organisations and on the edges of the state security forces, who were doing very well out of the violence. Many lawyers, for example, had earned vast sums of money out of defending people in the Troubles.

There were also many businessmen who gained financially from having a big brother behind them when they had troubles in their businesses. Nightclub owners, for example, could call on the services of the IRA or the UDA to back them if there was a dispute on their premises. Northern Ireland was a seedy world where the strong succeeded despite the violence, and only the weak felt the pain of it.

Nonetheless, there were many who benefited from the conflict.

A friend called one night with his older brother, who was visiting Belfast to collect a relative from the airport. It was the kind of visit that seemed a little unusual, but was not so unusual that you would remark upon it.

My friend sat down in the living room, and his brother beside him. We were chatting about this and that, and having a cup of coffee, when my friend's brother asked me something very interesting.

'What do you think of the Knights of Columbanus?' he asked nonchalantly, but with a level of disguised intent that wasn't very well disguised. My only thought was that my friend's brother was a Knight.

I had my moment to tell one of them exactly what I thought of their organisation.

'They're just like the Masons, up to everything,' I said.

He was very disappointed, as if I had hurt him personally.

'Oh, if that's the way you feel,' he said. Then he stopped speaking and excused himself as he got up and walked towards our front door.

It was clear that he had an agenda and it involved him talking to me about membership of the Knights of Columbanus. He had tried to be discreet, but my outright hostility to the Knights had destroyed any semblance of discretion in his mission. He had walked out in a huff.

I was glad that I had said what I said. I had spoken from the heart because I knew that some Knights were using their organisation to hide their anti-British and anti-Protestant prejudices, and because some of them were active members of the IRA establishment, who governed areas of the North with an iron fist.

I hated these Knights with a passion because they were the real enemies of the Church, wheeling and dealing and using the Church for cover for their activities. I hated them because they would have it said that they were upright Christian men when in actual fact they were cowards who hadn't the guts to put on the uniform of the priests in the fight with injustice.

They had corrupted the Church in some ways, but mostly they were just a pain in the ass because you had to look over your shoulder in the North to see if your friends or enemies were really Knights.

But when my friend left, not long after his brother, I had to examine my meeting with this particular Knight. It had come at a timely moment. I was in the middle of a tax investigation that probably involved a pillar of the community, also known as a possible Knight of Columbanus, who had secreted almost two million pounds on behalf of the IRA.

My brother's friend seemed too annoyed that I had bad-mouthed the Knights. It also seemed that he had come to recruit me. Why would he leave so quickly, saying that 'if that's the way you feel'? 'If that's the way you feel, then why should I attempt to recruit you to the Knights of Columbanus,' was what he meant to say.

The Knights were on my case. They were attempting to protect the reputation of one of their members, or they were attempting to recruit me to their ruthless and vicious conspiracy. They wanted me to join the Knights rather than have me as a risk to the reputation of their businessman friend, big Tom Brennan, or as a risk to the safety of their members, who could be big Tom and my boss Sean.

It was a scary thought. Big Tom and Sean would inevitably want some coverage now that I had practically admitted that I thought that the offshore accounts were a front for laundered IRA money.

It would have been nice for them to recruit me to the Knights of Columbanus. At the very least it would ensure that there was a little pressure on me to do the right thing by other Knights. That meant that I would keep a protective eye out for Sean and big Tom Brennan.

At the very most, they could use the professional terrorists among the Knights to apply pressure on me not to do anything other than what I was told to do in the case. There was the pressure to conform and the fear of the consequences of not conforming.

But it was a very interesting visit from my friend's older brother.

Sean seemed angry at me the following day. At the very least, it seemed that he was fed up with me. I wondered about the Knight who had visited me. Perhaps Sean already knew that I had turned him down.

It was not impossible that this was the case. All it would have taken was a phone call. I had to be extra careful not to allow myself to lose focus on the tax investigation. But I was disappointed with Sean.

Sean had recruited me to the firm almost four years beforehand. He had been my first boss in a meaningful sense. But, more than that, he had been like a father figure to me since I began to work with him. He had always been positive with me, excusing any misdemeanours, and encouraging me to achieve my potential.

He had always ensured that I got the best quality of work going in the office, and that I faced challenging and varied work which would ease my way through the accountancy exams.

He was my mentor and my role model. The first job was a difficult time for any young graduate, and Sean had been with me through thick and thin, and I looked upon him as someone who would always see me right while I worked for him. He had always been fair with me.

I was disappointed now for the first time in my working life. Sean had let me down by involving me in a tax investigation that implicated me in a conspiracy to hide the fact that we were dealing with IRA hunger strike money.

I was now so deeply involved in that conspiracy purely by my presence in the office as the most experienced member of staff, and as someone, who being reasonably intelligent, could not plead ignorance to the fact that it was a deeply suspicious case.

I knew it was IRA money. I couldn't deny that. The visit by the Knight of Columbanus merely confirmed to me both that members of that organisation helped the IRA and that the IRA were trying to ensure that I didn't create any problems.

They were probably saying all sorts of things about me, now that I had shot down the Knights. They were probably saying that I was a dogged bastard, who had shown no compassion for a Knight who was in trouble, or big Tom Brennan as I knew him. But I had also shown no regard for Sean in their eyes, and that may have created more alarm in them.

Sean had given me the opportunity to begin my career and yet I was showing no loyalty to him. But loyalty for an employer was for me a loyalty that had limits.

He had at times shown me no loyalty, as when I had asked for a pay-rise during my first year in the firm because my housing benefit had been cut. He had turned me down, and starved me of cash at a time when I really needed it. He came back to me at that time and told me that the other partners wouldn't agree to it, as it would have meant that other trainees would want extra money.

I lived in Belfast at that time, and the other trainees lived with their parents in county Tyrone, and so the refusal rankled with me. I was in poverty while the partners, who had benefited from Margaret Thatcher's 1988 tax cutting budget, which had also cut my housing benefit, had been getting fat on their excess incomes.

I had also memories of how Sean had failed in his duty to get my increased trainee salary paid to me in a timely fashion, and of how that salary increase was delayed so much that I had become tense that I was to forever remain without it.

The increased salary had come as a result of a merger of our medium-sized firm with a very large accountancy practice where trainees were paid better salaries.

There were, of course, other partners in the firm, who would be shocked if I told them what Sean was up to. I was not part of their framework and I had no loyalty to them, and so I did not believe that it was the right road to go down.

They would have gone straight to the police in order to minimise potential damage to the reputation of the firm, something to which Sean seemed totally oblivious. But the other partners in Belfast were mainly Protestants, and the fact was that they might not have trusted my motives.

In fact, to go down that route was to go down the route of going directly to the police. It amounted to the same thing. I would have been in trouble.

Nonetheless, I was already in trouble. The Knights of Columbanus would not let things sit. They would do something else to attempt to exert some influence on me. It was even possible at this stage that they would throw caution to the wind and have me executed for non-cooperation with their membership.

It was possible, but it was not likely. The first thing that would happen if I was shot was that my desk would have been searched and my place of employment scrutinised to see if there was any reason why anyone would want me dead. The police would be swarming around our office looking for clues.

Even a sniffer-dog with a bad flu would have scented a policeman's paradise on my desk. A blind man would have seen a fusion of clues in my possession and, even if Sean removed them, the police would examine timesheets to see what jobs I had been working on. It would be very foolish in the extreme for republicans to attempt to move on me.

In reality, I was pretty safe if I stood still, so to speak, and made no wrong moves. One wrong move on my part and the subsequent crisis would result in someone being shot, probably me.

Nevertheless, I was not afraid. I had a feeling of tension, but not fear. But I was a young and healthy man, and I had felt the tension before. I had felt it intensely during my study for the professional exams, but it had gone away in time.

This time, however, I was no longer a student. I had no longer to put up with other people's inconveniences. I was my own man. I had a choice not to be stressed.

I decided to take some time off. I asked Sean for two weeks' holiday, saying that I was feeling some tension.

'We'd be a bit stuck if anything happened here,' he said, thinking about it. Something must have triggered a thought in his mind that said that it might be beneficial to him if I left for a while, since he agreed to my request. 'Enjoy your holiday,' he smiled as if he had the perfect plan thought out.

I knew what he was thinking. If he got me out of the way he might be able to get the tax investigation completed before I got back. Or he could even switch my work to someone else who might not be as discerning as me. Either way, Sean didn't seem to think that he would need me on the job again.

   Needless to say, I, too, was happy at that thought.

Chapter Eight

'Jesus, John!' Bernie yelped as she tried to mop up some of the wine I had spilled on the restaurant table.

I was nervous as I told her that I was going away for a couple of weeks. She was asking questions that I couldn't answer. A nervous twitch of my right arm had knocked over my glass of wine.

'What's wrong, John?' she wondered. 'You don't seem like your usual self.'

'I'm clumsy like this sometimes,' I replied, relying on her lack of knowledge of me in order to get my white lie past her.

'No,' she said, 'you're worried about something.'

I was trying to be sophisticated, but Bernie wasn't fooled by my disposition. Her perceptiveness was revealing. It showed that no matter how far up the social ladder you progressed the simple things remained the same. A straightforward person like Bernie wasn't fooled by my façade.

I could hide it from people like Sean, a hard-working chartered accountant, but I couldn't hide it from a restaurant waitress like Bernie. I felt some tension and I had to deal with it. I had to deal with Bernie first.

I waited until we had left the restaurant, and were strolling back to her flat, before I told her that I had some problems at work. I told her that there were some dodgy accounts going through the office and I was afraid that it might destroy my reputation.

'Is it the IRA?' she wondered, shocking me with her guess.

'As a matter of fact, it is,' I said. 'But you must never mention this to anybody.'

'My brother has connections,' Bernie said meekly. 'He could help you.'

'I don't think so,' I said. 'But thanks for offering.'

'Why not?' she wondered.

'Because this isn't about some local community organisation,' I told her. 'This is about big business and the mob.'

'The mafia?' Bernie wondered.

'Yeah,' I replied, resignedly. 'It's strange but true.'

'Sure they're all Italian, the mafia,' Bernie said, with a naïve sigh.

I laughed. Bernie was so innocent at times, and yet so advanced at other times.

'What?' she said.

'This mafia is all Irish,' I smiled.

As we got to her apartment, I put my arms around her and we kissed. I liked Bernie. She had character, even if she was a little slow at times. We lived in different worlds. Her mafia were the thugs who had ruled west Belfast for a couple of decades, and who were turning it into a lawless zone. My mafia was different. They would like to call themselves civilised men, who were upright citizens fighting a just war against the British government. Nevertheless, behind the façades were wicked men who would steal your soul and try to sell it back to you.

They were so perverted that they would kill you as soon as look at you. In short, they were businessmen.

I meant business with Bernie that night. We had sex a few times. It was really interesting, due to her large breasts, but it wasn't as pleasurable as I anticipated it would be. It was always the same with sex. It was never as enjoyable as one might think it should be. It was always a bit disappointing.

Bernie had me really turned on to begin with. I considered going to the toilet and masturbating so that I wouldn't give her the first easy one. But I decided against it.

She was a horny bitch. However, sex also seemed to be routine to her, as if she had conquered it and didn't need to learn anything new. I really hated that bartender who had used an eighteen-year-old girl for sex, because I knew that that was where Bernie had been taught all the moves.

The one thing I really hated was the taking of someone's innocence. I would never do anything with girls unless they had done it before. If they hadn't, there were other ways to spend the night with them. If they had had sexual relations before, I would have been in there like a shot. It was paradoxical thinking in some ways, but it was not hypocrisy. I hated hypocrisy.

I hated the hypocrisy of the godfathers of the IRA, who would sometimes be sitting at the front of chapels on Sunday, with their wives and children, while other young men engaged in the same battle were incarcerated in prisons.

They were true hypocrites. Some of them would even read at mass as if they really knew what the Church stood for, and yet in their daily lives they were helping to organise a campaign of violence that was so brutal that it beggared belief that they were able to live with themselves.

I admired their ability to get away with their double lives. There was a certain romance at being able to fool everyone into believing that you were an upright citizen, perhaps with many friends from the Protestant section of the community, and yet you were in reality fighting a vicious war against these same people and their forces of law and order.

There was, of course, equal hypocrisy on the Protestant side, where having Catholic friends could be regarded as a cover for membership of extremely violent paramilitary organisations. There was even hypocrisy in the forces of law and order of the state where anti-Catholic bigotry was rife and massaging of the rules was commonplace.

The police massaged the rules to let certain people off with offences. These people were usually Protestants, but not always. I had a Catholic friend, who had worked for a Protestant firm, whose owner and my friend's mentor was a member of the Orange Order, and he got off on a couple of occasions with speeding fines because of this connection.

The police also massaged the rules to ensure that they came down like a tonne of bricks on Catholics who had no connections. The police harassed and beat members of my community into submission. Sometimes they took them to Castlereagh holding centre in Belfast, where they interrogated paramilitary suspects with extreme vigour and devastating effects.

The police were brutal because they didn't know any better. A disproportionately large number of senior officers in the RUC were said to be members of the Free Presbyterian Church, a protestant sect formed by the Reverend Ian Paisley. They were the kind of religious fundamentalists who held that the laws of man were the same as the laws of God. I disagreed with that analysis, and I knew that many of these same Free Presbyterians would believe likewise if the Catholics were in the ascendancy. There would be no problem then about using violence to undermine the state.

But the IRA paramilitaries were the real hypocrites. They were fomenting hostilities between the communities in the North. Therefore they had to justify the campaigns of violence on the basis that Catholics were gaining something out of it.

What the Catholics were gaining out of it was a mafia mindset. These businessmen, with their connections to the Gaelic Athletic Association and the Catholic Church, were acting in the true mafia tradition of Hollywood.

Donations to the Church were undertaken regularly to keep their consciences clear, and to keep them sweet with Catholic priests who might have to give them a reference in difficult times.

The GAA would give them a cover for any activities that might be seen as being conspiratorial in relation to the dismantling of the state of Northern Ireland.

It was a nasty business. They were trying to take down a part of the United Kingdom, and their violence needed to be extreme. It was.

Nonetheless, what was happening under the surface was that the mafia was taking control of Catholic areas through brutal force. Personalities were developing in the mafia and they were asserting their values on the people of those areas.

I woke in Bernie's apartment the following morning. I had a shower and made my way to my own digs, where I changed my shirt, which had been stained by the wine I spilled the night before. Then I made my way to work.

I was tired when I arrived, but I was able to do what I was supposed to do. I had plenty of reserves of energy. I could sometimes stay awake for an entire night and still perform my duties in the office. I would be wrecked when I got home the following evening, and I would have to go to bed early, but I was still able to do my job.

That day was my last day at work for a couple of weeks, and I intended to ensure that there was nothing left outstanding that would be used against me when I returned. By the end of the day I was in control of the jobs on my desk, and I filed the files away in the knowledge that there would be no problems in relation to nearly all my jobs.

The only job that had the potential to cause problems was big Tom Brennan's, whose file I looked over the previous night at home before meeting Bernie. It might require to be acted upon quickly and the client might require information from it so it was best to leave it with my boss. But I forgot since I was tired, and I assumed that it was in a filing cabinet.

I drove straight back to my digs after work. I was exhausted but I wanted to get home to Derry before darkness fell. I lay down for a moment on the couch in the living-room and closed my eyes. It felt like only a moment, but I woke three hours later in the darkened room with the television blaring beside me.

I decided to stay in Belfast that night. I felt quite sprightly after my sleep, and when I had ordered and eaten a takeaway, I was in the mood for going out.

It was after ten o'clock when I got to a pub. I stood at the bar, not seeing anyone I knew, and drank a pint of Guinness.

After about twenty minutes, an acquaintance approached me. He was accompanied by his friend, who seemed big into the GAA by the way he wore a Tyrone GAA jersey under his v-neck jumper.

'How's things?' Kieran asked.

'Can't complain,' I said. 'I'm off on a couple of weeks holiday.'

'Where are you going?' he asked.

'Don't know yet,' I replied. 'I'm not going anywhere for a few days.'

'I hear Crete is good at this time of year,' said Adrian, or "Aids" as he introduced himself with a smug smile and a warning that he "shoots venom". Kieran's friend seemed a bit of an oddball.

'I'm not going that far,' I said. Kieran looked at me. It seemed that he had intent behind his eyes.

'Where are you going?' he said, half-arrogantly.

I laughed. 'What the fuck do you want to know for?' I asked.

'Somebody asked us to have a word with you,' Aids said, with his heavy Tyrone accent. I was now getting the impression that Aids was there for a reason, and that he was not well known around Belfast. In other words, he was there to make some kind of threat.

'What did they want you to say to me?' I wondered, restraining my anger.

'Just be very careful,' Aids said. 'That's all.'

'Oh!'

'We mean, very careful,' Aids added, 'that you don't talk to the wrong people. You know the kind of things that can happen on these holidays.' He prodded me on the chest, and attempted to grip my jumper.

I pushed him back.

'Don't worry,' I said. 'I never talk to the wrong people.'

'Don't push me,' Aids said threateningly.

'Aids,' Kieran interjected.

'What?' Aids said. Aids was big and bulky, but I wasn't afraid of him. He would go down like a tonne of bricks if I moved on him.

Nevertheless, he pulled back at Kieran's instigation.

'What's this about, boys?' I asked, attempting to make them look stupid because there was no way that they would be aware of the tax investigation.

'You know what it's about,' Kieran answered arrogantly.

'Yeah, but you don't,' I said angrily. 'You're just the brawn. I only deal with the brains.'

'You tell us what it's about then,' Aids said, his voice still issuing threats.

'No,' Kieran said.

'Yes,' Aids said.

Kieran grabbed Aids by the arm. 'We're out of here now.'

'It's more than your life's worth if I told you,' I said, my *coup de grace* making big Aids even more angry. He lunged at me and tried to grab my jumper again.

'Who to fuck do you think you are?' he roared. 'Do you know who I am?'

At this point two bouncers, who had been hovering behind Aids, moved in and grabbed the big muscle-bound idiot. They weren't interested in his excuses, as they moved him quickly through the bar and out the front door.

I knew that that was the only possible outcome if big Aids got agitated. He could have thumped me, but he was probably so hung up about the disciplines of the IRA that he would have waited until I struck him first. I wasn't going to do that. He was a big bastard, and he might have killed me. I wasn't going to give the IRA that opportunity.

Kieran whispered in my ear as the bouncers moved away from us, dragging big Aids.

'We'll be watching you,' he said.

I knew that he was serious. It wasn't the kind of threat you could take lightly. They would be watching me. There was no doubt about that.

They would be watching to ensure that I made no wrong moves. They would be watching to ensure that I didn't go to the police or to a public representative with my story.

I had ruled the police out. They were not to be trusted as they represented everything that I wanted changed in the state of Northern Ireland.

But I could still go to a public representative. A senior SDLP politician was probably the best route. I didn't know what could be done but something had to be done, or else these people would destroy me.

Yet I felt strangely uncompelled to go to anyone. I felt that I could handle it. All they could do was observe me. They could not afford to harm me.

Nonetheless I was faced with a moral dilemma. How was I to deal with the fact that IRA money was being given over to the British Exchequer? Was it my problem? If it was, then what action should I take to maximise the damage to the IRA, the enemies of good people everywhere?

They were only questions at that moment and, as I strolled back to my home in Belfast that night, I had no answers.

Chapter Nine

It was a beautiful winter's day as I drove back to Derry the next morning. It was even more beautiful since it was a Saturday and there was no work to go to. It was doubly beautiful because I had the next two weeks off work.

I was happy as I drove up the M2 motorway. It was easy driving, the kind that made you feel that you were in control in your own world.

But I wasn't in control of my own world. I had been, more or less, threatened the previous night by junior members of the IRA. I assumed that they didn't know why they were threatening me, other than that they were told some spurious story by their superior officers.

I wondered what story they had been told. Perhaps they had been told something about me talking to the "wrong people" about something totally unrelated to my job. They had been very insistent that I didn't talk to the "wrong people".

What "wrong people" were they? Were they afraid of me talking to the police, or were they afraid that I might inform members of their organisation in Derry that a big shot member, namely Tom Brennan, had pissed two million pounds of hunger strike money down the toilet through his own carelessness.

That would be really revealing for some members of the Derry city brigade of the IRA. They would be very interested in that story. They would want to know exactly what happened and exactly what kind of idiot sat with two million pounds in bank accounts in his name while his businesses were just about able to turn over a profit.

They would want to know who authorised the lodging of over five hundred thousand pounds to an individual's offshore bank account in one single year, creating an impossibility for him to explain it away as the surplus of his trading.

Ordinary members of the IRA would want to know what was going on in the accounting sections of the organisation. While they were bursting their guts for the cause there were those who, with the stroke of a pen, were prepared to sign away the proceeds of their dead comrades' efforts.

Hunger strikers had given their lives to breath new life into their organisation, which was almost dead when they began their protests in late 1980. In 1981, after the failure of their first strike, they had starved themselves to their deaths over the course of several months, creating a well of sympathy all over the world.

Everyone knew of their cause after that. Everyone knew of the name of Bobby Sands, the first hunger-striker and the leader of the IRA in the H-Blocks, who had even been elected as the MP for Fermanagh and South Tyrone before his death in May 1981.

For a time everyone knew of the names of all ten hunger strikers. They were all blessed men, some of whom had been elected to Dail Eireann during the summer of 1981, when there had been a general election in the Republic of Ireland.

I recalled living through the period of the hunger strikes. It created enormous division in the Catholic community. Most people supported the hunger strikers themselves, but relatively few supported the IRA.

I didn't know whether to support the starving men. I felt so stretched by the enormous emotional upheaval that was entailed by what they were doing. There were so many contradictions between what the hunger strikers said they stood for, and what I saw them really standing for in my community.

I knew there were people like big Tom Brennan in the IRA, with their big golden Mercedes Benzes. There was no point in believing that people like big Tom Brennan were idealists, who would starve themselves to death for others. They would simply laugh at the very suggestion.

In that sense the hunger strikers were used to give sustenance to the non-combatants in the IRA hierarchy, a few of whom may well have been against the hunger strikes, but many of whom were prepared to live with the consequences of millions of pounds in receipts to their cause.

There was no point being an idealist while at the very core of your organisation was a cancerous cluster of godfathers, who didn't give the slightest damn about your idealism. The hunger strikers were used all right, and some of the cash they earned for the cause was frittered away by a stupid man.

In a sense the hunger strikers had died for evil. They died as a result of a corrupt idealism that said it was all right to kill, but to expect that everyone else would still recognise the justice of their cause.

In reality, everyone could identify with their plight. They had been refused the right to be treated as prisoners of war. They weren't allowed to wear their own clothes, for example, and they were being treated like petty criminals.

Most Nationalists felt that they should be treated with dignity and respect for their humanity. That meant that they should be treated as, at least, special category prisoners, if not fully recognised as prisoners of war under the Geneva Convention.

But what I couldn't understand was why it should matter to them what the enemy, as they regarded the state they were fighting, thought of them. If the enemy treats you like a criminal, it doesn't make you a criminal. Even if the enemy treats you as a prisoner of war, giving you special status and privileges, you may still not warrant such a status or such privileges.

The IRA inmates seemed obsessed with what the British said about them. They seemed to care about how the British defined them. It was surely a case of showing far too much respect to the enemy, an enemy they had tried to shoot and bomb to death outside the prison.

To me their struggle for rights inside the prison was about prison politics. They were afraid to be regarded as common criminals by "the screws", or the prison warders. It seemed like a simple matter about a clash between the system they were incarcerated by and their own insecurities about who they were.

If they really believed that they were prisoners of war, then it wouldn't have mattered that the British prison system, a part of the British political system they were trying to destroy, was attempting to define them as criminals.

The reality was that many of the young people who had got caught up in the war with the British were not committed to the concept of being prisoners of war. They would rather that they were at home and wanted to get home as quickly as they could. Sensing that morale would be undermined if they didn't fight the prison issue, some IRA leaders stoked up their prisoners to rebel.

There was, of course, the issue that what went on inside the prisons would be reflected outside the prisons. If the British broke the IRA inside the prisons, then they could break them outside the prisons.

That might in turn lead to the demoralisation of the entire Nationalist community, and the defeat of its objectives. So the IRA decided to make a stand inside the prisons.

In my opinion, it doesn't get anymore stupid than that. The IRA attempted to fight a war inside the prisons, demonstrating an insecurity that they needed to be told by their enemy that they really are their enemy, and not criminals. It was the kind of stupidity that had only been matched by big Tom Brennan with his offshore accounts.

It may be argued that the IRA won the hunger strike issue due to the massive publicity it received. However, it wasn't as simple as that.

In the late 1970's, many republican prisoners went on the blanket protest when they refused prison issue clothes, and sat naked in their cells covered by blankets.

Then some republican prisoners began to smear their excrement on the walls of their cells. It was an undignified protest that made the men out to be animals. Added to this lack of dignity, there was the fact that they were trying to outwit a notoriously fascist British regime while they were in fact prisoners of that regime.

It was utter folly to go down that road. The IRA were in effect dehumanising the prisoners to fight a war inside the prisons that they hadn't been able to win outside. They were making their own prisoners so desperate that they would do anything eventually to win the issue.

The cumulative effect of being on the blanket, and then on "the dirty protest", as it was called during the four years it lasted, had cancelled out any attachment to reality that these prisoners may have had. The prisoners were in a psychosis, which was fuelled by their desperate methods.

They were ultimately ripe for exploitation when the suggestion of a hunger strike came along. It was, of course, the prisoners' suggestion. It was their choice, but the leadership outside the prison should never have allowed them to embark on a collision course with the state inside those brutal prisons.

However, it wasn't pure idealism that had motivated the prisoners. They were in psychoses and they were desperate, but they were not idealistic. Their psychoses may well have been formed under the influence of "republican theology", which may well have some idealism at its core, but that wasn't my kind of idealism.

Four years of smearing your own shit on the walls of your cell could not have a good effect on you. It was monstrous, dehumanising and detached the prisoners from reality. The mantra of the republican songs and the poems and the idealism of a common cause had enlivened a part of them that no human being could ever imagine.

If they had have been asked to go on hunger strike on the first day that they entered the prison, the same ten hunger strikers who had died would not have been able to generate a starvation lasting more than a few days. They simply wouldn't have had the energy or the sheer determination.

Four years of sitting naked in a cell with only a blanket to take away the smell of the excrement on the walls was not how human beings should choose to protest. They should especially not choose to do it in a prison run by their enemies. It was like mice, throwing their collective heads in the experimental laboratories that were their home, and telling their "employers" that they were no longer going to conform. The "employers" would simply destroy them.

The republican prisoners were in a laboratory of a sort, and the prison system, their "employers", was simply going to destroy them. At the very least, they were going to watch as the prisoners destroyed themselves.

In another sense the hunger strikers had chosen one of the vehicles of Christian sacrifice, fasting, to win their case. But it was the opposite of how Christ intended it. Christ said that we were to give in private, so that our left hand doesn't know what our right hand is doing.

Also in the case of fasting, Jesus had set the example of fasting in secret. He went out into the desert for forty days and forty nights on his own. There were to be no witnesses as he fasted. It was a private matter between him and God. And it is written that what is seen in private by God will be rewarded.

The hunger strikers had shown an almost Pharisee-like attitude to fasting. Not only did they not do it in private and keep it between themselves and God, they had actually done it in front of the entire world as if to seek the praise of men for their efforts.

I could forgive the hunger strikers. They simply didn't know any better. They were in republican psychoses and they were desperate. But I couldn't forgive the Pharisee element behind them. There were priests who were lapping it up, I'm sure. There were men like Tom Brennan, possible Knights of Columbanus, who were living off the backs of these deluded men.

No-one gives their life for prison uniforms, or any of the other five demands of the prisoners. The hunger strikers gave their lives because they wanted to be free, just like any other prisoner in the same circumstances. Who really gives a damn what the British government thinks of them, when you're in prison for trying to destroy them and their presence in Ireland?

Gerry Adams, the Sinn Fein president, and many of the Sinn Fein leadership were against the hunger strikes because they thought that the men would be defeated. But he said in a recent interview that the British government attempted to criminalize the prisoners, and the prisoners ended up criminalizing the British government.

It was a high-risk strategy. The prisoners by all rationality should have lost their protest. It seems that it was not good for publicity for them to lose. It was not good for Sinn Fein or for the IRA outside the prisons.

Nonetheless, in my mind they had lost the protest by going to their deaths over very little. The republican movement lost because they gave the prisoners no leadership, and left them to fight their own battles within the system.

They had created a new religion with its very own martyrs. And yet these martyrs had not been born in dignity, but in four years of smearing their own shit on the walls of their cells. They were undignified martyrs, engaged in an undignified protest, that had ended with them taking their own lives in a very public fast driven by the desire to impress man and not God.

My stomach churned afterwards when I heard of conversations between the British Prime Minister, Margaret Thatcher, and the late Cardinal Tomas O'Fiaich. O'Fiaich had attempted to tell Margaret Thatcher to get out of Ireland in return for him telling the hunger strikers to call off their fast.

It was the attitude of a true Pharisee, hiding in the high Church, and playing with people's lives. But what else could he do? It wouldn't have been right either if he had undermined the prisoners' protest while they were finally putting the British under pressure after years of failure.

In reality, he could have told Margaret Thatcher to get lost, and done it publicly, while at the same time, he could have acted in the interests of his own people. Those interests were not served by the hunger strikes. They created division and undermined the Christian values of his flock.

Instead, Cardinal O'Fiaich acted at the very least as a bystander, witnessing the spectacle of his own Church being scythed down the middle. He witnessed a schism in the Catholic faith right before his eyes, and he let it happen because he wanted to be so clever with the British government.

He wanted to impress the big Tom Brennans of this world with his fervent Nationalism, and his desire to be with the boys to their very deaths. O'Fiaich was a clever man academically, but he had no street wisdom.

He didn't realise that he was being shunted by the Gerry Adams of this world, who believed that "republican theology" was superior to Catholic theology. It was a case of him not knowing, since that was the way he was. I didn't believe that he would consciously create the circumstances of the demise of his own Church. He simply didn't realise that he had to protect his flock in those dire circumstances.

In that sense he should never have been the Cardinal. He should have stayed in academia, and let a more astute leader lead his flock.

People like big Tom Brennan read the signals from men like Cardinal O'Fiaich, and conveyed them to the great unwashed of the republican movement. Their war was just in the eyes of the Church, they concluded.

The Church wouldn't say it publicly, they murmured, but a time would come when they would switch their loyalties from the establishment parties such as the SDLP to the republican movement. Sinn Fein vice-president, Martin McGuinness, said as much in the 1980s.

Big Tom Brennan was probably lapping it up at this time, receiving, as he did, hundreds of thousands of pounds in American money within months of the deaths of the ten brave, but foolhardy, souls.

They had ultimately died so that big Tom Brennan could squeeze conscience and hate money out of the Irish-American community. They had died for Ireland, and their gravestones would forever recognise their deeds, but they had died so that others may die, not live.

They had died so that the funds would flow to the republican movement. They had died so that Sinn Fein could contest elections, and that the IRA could fight the noble fight with the British.

At the time of the tax investigation, in early 1991, there was no sense that the hunger strikers had died for peace, but there were apparently moves being made then to bring the IRA campaign to an end. This was said to be because Sinn Fein had decided that they would be more successful with their political strategy, a strategy born out of the hunger strikes, and the election of Bobby Sands as a MP on his deathbed.

Nevertheless, it was a case of Sinn Fein being hoisted by their own petard, since they could never have sustained an electoral strategy while fighting a military campaign. As the hunger strikes ended, Sinn Fein had been talking consistently about fighting with "the ballot box in one hand and the Armalite in the other". Clearly, they didn't realise that this was not possible.

Clearly, they had been caught out.

They had been caught out just as big Tom Brennan had been caught out.

Chapter Ten

Derry was buzzing that Saturday night. I was really enjoying myself since it was the first chance I had had in weeks to get away from the pressure of the tax investigation. More importantly, the feeling of being free from the office and away from Belfast, where all my troubles lay, was enthralling.

It was a happy moment, and I had had only a few of those in the previous weeks. I almost felt that I could discard any fears that the IRA would try to get me now that I was on my home patch, and I knew all the faces around me.

The bar was noisy and jubilant as if there had been a football match on earlier in the night. Perhaps there had been. There were FA Cup matches played that day, and perhaps one of them had been live on television. I didn't know.

I had had a few pints in the company of my friend Brian and Danny, a local solicitor. The conversation was quiet due to the noise levels in the bar. We were going to go elsewhere after a while, the noise having reached intolerable levels.

Then, all of a sudden a group of men got up from their table and made their way to the door, and things began to quieten down. We could talk and I was glad.

I wasn't glad for long, however, as the conversation became a bit obscure between Danny and me.

'What would you really like most now?' he asked.

'Bernie to arrive in so that I could have a night of passion,' I replied jocularly.

'Ah, fuck!' Danny said. 'What about in your career?' Danny seemed perturbed that I had not taken his initial question seriously enough.

'I would like a salary hike,' I said, continuing to be unserious just to annoy him.

'That can be arranged,' he smiled.

'What do you mean?' I said, angry that he thought he had control over any part of my life.

'I'm just saying,' Danny said, 'that you might want to move back to Derry some day, and I may be able to help.'

'No,' I protested. 'You meant something more than that.'

'I did?' he gasped. 'What do you mean?'

'You're up to something,' I said. 'I know you well enough to know that you're up to something.'

Danny just smiled and moved back into the crowd of friends who had gathered in our corner of the bar. He began to speak to someone and I was lost for words. I wanted to grab him and throw him on the floor so that I could interrogate him with a few boots to his mouth.

But I was not violent by nature. It was just the stress of dealing with the situation. It was so profoundly disturbing to find that people you knew were now showing the colours of their loyalty to another agenda.

These people were Provos. It was not uncommon for solicitors to have strong sympathies for the cause of the IRA, but with Danny you hitherto always felt that he had loyalty to you first. That was the theory anyway. The reality was that I had always suspected Danny of being a Provo.

In a sense he fitted the profile. He wandered from group to group, making friends here and there, and he never seemed to be entirely comfortable in one group. He was at times a deeply unhappy man underneath a façade of always wanting to go that bit further for a little fun.

He was a mixed up kid in some senses. In other senses he was as shrewd as a fox. Nonetheless, he wore his shrewdness on his sleeve as if to say that no-one could be as smart as him. And he was smart. That was why I now suspected him of attempting to send me a message.

The message was clear: if I wanted to come back to Derry to live in a few years time, then the mob could facilitate it.

Derry was a strange place in accountancy terms. But then so was Belfast, as I had learned in the previous month. But Derry was largely Catholic, and businessmen, especially young businessmen, tended to be prepared to give their support to armies since sometimes change comes too slowly through the normal channels.

There was so much interference in the development of Derry by outsiders that it was assumed the unionists and the British government were still attempting to rule it with subterfuge long after their writ had run its course.

There had been a Catholic majority in Derry for over a hundred years and, as the civil rights campaigns of the late 1960's began, about 70% of the population was Catholic. That didn't matter to the unionists. The corporation had a Protestant majority, due to a gerrymander of local electoral boundaries, and they were backed by an equally perverse government of Northern Ireland in Stormont.

Derry had given birth to the civil rights movement in a real sense since it was the second city of the Northern Ireland state, and the injustices there were so great that it was going to take a very long time for them to be rectified. That process began in 1968 when a march on October 5th was beaten off the streets by the police.

There was turbulence in Derry after that. Civil rights protestors vied with members of the republican movement for attention and the house of cards that was the Northern Ireland parliament was eventually tumbled over.

Young Catholics tended to support the IRA, and there grew up a generation of young people with IRA sympathies. The IRA were seen as liberators. They were seen as ordinary lads fighting a brave war against a powerful enemy, an enemy who had been complicit in the denial of their people civil rights.

The unionists had kept the Catholic citizens poor, and living in hovels, in order to maintain the unionist state. Whole families had lived in one room in houses around Derry city before the Troubles. Mothers, fathers and children had been humiliated to keep the Orange state alive.

There was a price to pay for that. The unionist state and the unnatural division of Ireland had to end. The unionist state had ended in 1972 after Bloody Sunday, when fourteen innocent men had been shot dead in Derry, and the Stormont parliament had been closed down.

After Bloody Sunday, the British army and their government became the enemy for the people of Derry. They had to be thrown out of Ireland once and for all. Derry was different to other Catholic areas of the North. The British, and not the unionists, were the prime enemy. The unionists had been defeated with the introduction of the reform of local government and the election in 1973 of a new Londonderry City Council, which had a large Catholic majority.

But the British had to be taught a lesson after Bloody Sunday. They were taught many lessons in the months and years after that. It culminated in the deaths of eighteen paratroopers, the regiment who had shot the innocent Derry men dead, in a booby-trapped bomb blast in Warrenpoint, county Down, in 1979.

Pints were downed in celebration in Derry that night. It was a massive coup for the IRA. The notorious Parachute regiment had been taught a harsh lesson by the IRA.

With all these lessons, you would think that every Derry person would have been by then a fervent supporter of the IRA. But it was much more complex than that.

The majority of Catholics in Derry were still very much opposed to violence in 1979, as in 1969. Violence was not the way to resolve the problem. The SDLP were in the ascendancy in Derry politics and remain to this day the largest party in Derry.

My feeling, like that of many of my fellow citizens, was that there had been too many Bloody Sundays, caused mainly by the IRA after Bloody Sunday itself, for violence to have any role to play in the resolution of the problems of the North of Ireland. I was opposed to violence, even if there was a twinkle in my eye on the night of the Warrenpoint massacre.

But there were others who saw no problem with violence, or advocating it "publicly"; or rather advocating it in private conversations that would not be overheard by the state forces or their "touts".

There was an undercurrent among the young professionals, who listened to the stories of how things used to be in Derry circles, and who concluded that it would never be like that again.

Their fathers or their mentors in the professions might have accepted that certain things were the way they were, and nothing could change them, but they could not. There was never going to be discrimination and injustice in Derry again.

They would support the use of violence, whenever necessary, to rid their society of the evil of British rule. There was no going back. All movement was to be in a forward direction.

It seemed on the surface to be a noble sentiment, and that these young hotheads were noble people. But that was far from the reality. Many of these people had poor self-images, and that was the reason why they felt it necessary to believe in the use of violence.

It made them seem sexy in the eyes of those they whispered to about their involvement. Some of them had a direct involvement; for others it was just a sympathetic ear.

Those who were involved tended to be intelligence officers gathering intelligence on the RUC and British army personnel they wanted to put to death. Others simply provided casual information to those they knew to be intelligence officers, or to other men or women who they knew to be in the IRA.

The hotheads were well-known. That was probably how they were recruited in the first place. They were seen out and about so much that it was reckoned that they would be able to get information on others without any questions needing to be asked.

For, not only did they target the RUC and the British army, they also targeted their own people who spoke out against the IRA. They were spies in a sense. You had to be careful what you said to these people. In fact, you had consequently to be careful what you said to any strangers who came into your company.

As a consequence of this caution, politics were rarely spoken between strangers or relative strangers, and it tended only to be spoken about among friends.

We lived in a strange society as I reached my maturity. There were spies on both sides of the fence, seeking to keep everyone outside their cliques guessing as to which side they were on. You had to be careful.

Politics inspired the strongest emotions in people in those days. People were beaten up for what they said about certain people. Republicans were noticeably sensitive about comments on them, or on their activities, or on their gangsterism.

Fights were sometimes the result of what had started as conversations about the Troubles and of how it was all getting out of hand. Republicans again were the most sensitive when it came to criticisms of them.

The young professionals had assumed an importance in the IRA after Bloody Sunday and over the years their importance grew such that they had acquired a controlling interest in the conspiracy by the early 1990's. The end result was that gangsters had begun to "rule" the town.

There was a clique in Derry, as in other cities, which liked to believe they had control of it. The IRA was this clique in Derry.

They were not simply thugs and killers though. They were men in grey and navy suits who had a financial interest in the city, and of how it developed, and who believed that they were the rightful government of the city. This was despite them not contesting elections.

A few were from among the old guard of the Nationalist Party who had been humiliated by the SDLP when the SDLP had first contested local elections in 1973. They were around about the time of Bloody Sunday and they felt greatly offended by the British army on that day.

The SDLP's response to the killings wasn't sufficiently strong for them. They took things into their own hands and decided that they were still the rightful leaders of their people.

Many of them had affiliations to the Roman Catholic Church, and had decided that their violence against the British amounted to a Just War. This concept was part of Roman Catholic theology as it was part of the theology of many other Christian religions. But these extreme Catholics believed that Bloody Sunday had been committed directly against Roman Catholics.

If there was ever justification for a Just War, then it existed after Bloody Sunday. The British had declared war on "the natives". They had effectively said: "Are you going to fight us or are you going to embarrass us?"

The civil rights marchers had embarrassed the British in international circles and, with the Cold War still raging, the Russians were able to use the television pictures to suggest that all was not well within the UK. It was a potent weapon. But the marchers stopped marching after Bloody Sunday.

The fighters took over, and in the middle of them was a bunch of Pharisee- supporting ex-Nationalists, motivated both by religion and by politics, who were going to score even with the British.

They didn't respect the SDLP. The SDLP ways had failed on Bloody Sunday. Now the ways of Catholic justice and Irish

Nationalist violence were going to amalgamate into a new rejuvenated force that was the IRA after that day.

In short, some of the Knights of Columbanus were coming on board. The motto of the Knights, "To restore all things in Christ", said it all. They were not designed for the purpose they were now embarking upon. They were doomed for defeat. But the Knights would have it that they were on the good side of the dispute, that they were in the right.

But wrong can never be right. Evil can never be good. There was neither justice nor good on their side as they proved throughout the course of the next several years after Bloody Sunday, when many went to their deaths as a result of their justice and their good.

That night, Danny approached me as I was leaving for a party. He was a little more relaxed after a few drinks, and his tongue was loosened a little.

'You have to ask yourself, do you really want to come back to Derry?' he said.

I grabbed him by the arm, and held tightly.

'What do you mean, Danny, me 'oul boy?' I asked. I didn't really give a damn what he was saying, the alcohol dulling my inhibitions.

'Let go,' he said.

'Why are you afraid?' I said, knowing that it was registering with him that I was hostile.

'I'm not afraid,' he roared, in a very unusual, masculine manner, which seemed to say that he really was petrified, and yet he was not prepared to admit it.

I laughed. 'You boys are all the same, you solicitors,' I said.

'How?'

'You want treated with kid gloves, but you won't treat anyone else with kid gloves,' I said.

'Get fucked now,' he said, 'or I'll sue you.'

We both laughed. I let him go, and he moved away.

'You be careful who you talk to,' he finally said when he was out of reach. 'I'm saying that as a friend.'

I laughed again. He was no friend of mine. The bastard.

Chapter Eleven

I had a sore head when I woke on Sunday morning. I walked to mass soon after I got up. I had a deep faith in God then, and I still do to some extent.

I also liked being part of the community as much as the next guy. The priests were usually good men, who had little to say about things like the Just War. They were not encouraging the IRA from the altar. In fact, I had heard them condemn violence many times from the altar.

They may have had all sorts of strong pro-Catholic Church dogma, as would be expected from priests, but they had kept much of this to themselves, so far as I could discern. Christ was the reason why I went to mass. So long as the priests were the purveyors of Christ's message, then I would be there.

I had all sorts of suspicions about certain priests over the years. I felt some of them were aware of the activities of certain members of the Knights of Columbanus, and they deliberately turned a blind eye to it. There were possibly some who even encouraged those renegade members of the Knights to carry out their activities, which they believed were in the interests of Catholics.

I never knew if there was anything to my suspicions. I often felt that I was just extrapolating my own strong views on the use of violence to others who should have held the same views, but didn't seem to. In other words, I was judging the priests by my standards, and they may well have had their own standards. They may well have had more influence in the matter of stopping the men of violence than I had with my strong views.

I listened to the priest's words during his sermon that day. I never usually listened. My mind was rarely sufficiently concentrated to listen very long to someone speaking about something that I had my own views on. Usually I kind of listened, with intermittent concentration and indifferent interest, to sentences that seemed to make sense.

The priest spoke about the dangers of drug abuse that day. I was interested since he talked about alcohol as a drug and I was wondering where he was coming from. It seemed after listening to him that it was just one of those sermons that needed to be said.

But towards the end of mass, as he was giving his blessing and letting us go on home, the priest came out with something unusual.

'Be careful who you talk to this week,' he said. He paused and then added: 'There's a lot of talk about drugs being sold in the parish and in the neighbouring parishes.'

I wasn't sure if this was yet another warning about being careful who I talked to. If it was, it was appalling. If it was just a coincidence, then perhaps I needed time to reflect on the state of my mind.

But for a moment I thought he was talking directly to me. Perhaps the priest was under the influence of the renegade Knights of Columbanus, and they were simply wheeling out the big-hitters to show that they had ways to get at me if I didn't do the right thing. Nonetheless, it seemed so outrageous. It was well beyond the pale.

I was outraged and yet I knew it could all be in my mind.

I decided to get out of town that day. I had thought that I would spend some relaxing time at home before embarking on a holiday, but that was not the way it was working out.

And this thing about drugs annoyed me. This was the other possibility, albeit one that I had ruled out, in relation to the hunger strike money. It could have come from drugs. The IRA was said to be involved in the drugs trade. Perhaps that was why the priest had talked about drug abuse in his sermon. However, that would have rendered the priest's warning to me satanic, and I couldn't see that in him. In fact, he didn't have it in him, I concluded, and that aspect was probably just a coincidence.

Nonetheless, the advice to be careful whom we talked to was so much of a coincidence that it simply could not have been a coincidence. It was real enough, I thought, after reflection.

They were trying to scare me, I thought. They wanted me to believe that they could get at me anywhere. But they weren't going to succeed in that. I was going to get away from them.

After lunch, I made my way to the outskirts of Derry, where I could be sure that I wasn't being followed. I drove around the back roads for a while to ensure that no-one was able to follow me, and when I was sure that I was on my own, I drove deep into county Donegal.

After an hour's drive, I stopped at a shrine near Kilmacrennan on the road to west Donegal. The shrine was called "Doon Well" and was mainly a healing well. There was also a mass rock, and a coronation stone for the ancient O'Donnell kings of Donegal.

It was an extremely interesting shrine. There was a certain beauty to it, as if it had all the elements of Irish history there in the one place.

There were the secular kings, who were installed by the Bishops of their time. There were the mass rocks, reflecting a time during the Penal Code of the 18th century when the Church had been driven underground by the British authorities, and made to say mass in hidden places away from the beaten track. And there was a healing well, where men and women had sought healing from the water of eternal life for as long as people could remember.

In a sense there were the remnants of the historic fathers of the nation, the sons of the Church, and the Holy Sprit of the well all in the one unique location. Father, Son and Holy Spirit, a trinity of forces all existed at that little shrine in the middle of nowhere.

I looked around me for God when I went there, which I usually only did when I was feeling the need to address my spiritual deficit. I felt that need at that moment, in early 1991, when the whole of Irish society seemed to be conspiring to bring about my downfall.

But they weren't, I sensed, trying to destroy me. That would not have served their purposes. They needed me to stay alive and well. Moreover, they needed me to stay alert and rational, rational in the sense that I was aware that they had me over a barrel if I decided to break their rules.

I looked around at the shrine and decided that there were no rules that they could hold me by. I had to decide what was right, and if I was to do that, I would have to feel right.

I felt better when I drank the mystical water of the healing well, which was probably as impure as any tap water. But it was deeply refreshing. I felt that I had cleansed myself.

I felt great as I ascended the small hill to the inauguration stone of the O'Donnell kings of Donegal. When I arrived there the wind was howling and the sun was shining brightly, on what was a beautiful winter's day. Then the rain started to come down lightly, then more strongly.

I held my hands up to heaven and felt nature. The sun, wind and rain were all hitting me at once, as if God was trying to tell me something. It was the most beautiful feeling. I could never conquer nature, but nature had the capacity to augment me and even make me into a part of God.

I was not afraid any longer. I was not confused. I was in control even in the very midst of the most terrifying powers that nature could throw at me.

Nature was powerful, but it could never destroy me unless I let it. I saw the investigation in Belfast in the same light. It could terrify me but it could never destroy me. I was in control. I was in charge.

The IRA could never really get at me. I was in the saddle and they were running on their feet after me. They could only attempt to scare me. They could not kill me.

In effect, I had the IRA by the balls. I knew it and they knew it. It was only a case of me dealing with the situation as I saw fit.

There was such beauty in county Donegal. It was a typical west of Ireland county in many ways, and the west of Ireland was so beautiful. Why was it so beautiful?

I had never asked that question before. I had always admired the beauty of Ireland along its western seaboard, but I had never wondered why.

Now, as I drove through the often desolate and bare countryside of Donegal, I thought I knew why. It was to do with the fact that there were so few people there. More than that, those who lived there were exceptionally good people. They were saintly and honest.

The west of Ireland was so beautiful since the people of the west of Ireland were so beautiful. It was to do with the lack of development, which was very apparent except in the coastal villages where tourism was strong.

Money made the world ugly. That was how God must see it, I thought. That was why he chose the rural, sparsely populated, and underdeveloped areas of the world for his great signals to the world.

He chose the village of Knock in the west of Ireland, where there had been apparitions of the Blessed Virgin in the 1800's, for signals to the Irish people, and to peoples everywhere, of his love for them. He wanted this beautiful west of Ireland to be the way the landscape was for all people, with its strong communities and its underdeveloped natural earth.

I couldn't get away from that fact while I was witnessing this beauty. God didn't want the world to identify with places such as the Isle of Man with its corrupt banking arrangements even if it had a beautiful terrain. No-one could possibly see the Isle of Man as beautiful in the same way as the west of Ireland simply because there was so much money and tourism there.

God wanted the world to be beautiful. He seemed to will us to keep the world beautiful. But he knew that it was our destiny to do our level best to attempt to destroy much of its beauty. Men like big Tom Brennan took the beauty out of our humanity. Entrepreneurs and capitalists would destroy mankind if they were allowed to.

God knew that. That's really why he sent his son. He gave us free will to do as we like, but He was also responsible in that He gave us His son to save the world from these merchants of evil.

The war on the destruction of the earth was the most important aspect of Christianity. If we were stewards of the earth, then our stewardship had to result in less destruction of the natural beauty of the world.

That would result in a lower likelihood that I would meet people like big Tom Brennan in my travels. That was a goal worth seeking. That was a challenge worth undertaking. If only I could get a Church which would tell developers and profiteers that they were wrong to tear up the natural beauty of the world.

The saving grace for the west of Ireland was that it had so few resources that these men could make profit from. That was why there were so few of them. They had moved away to find profitable ventures elsewhere.

There was great poverty in Donegal as a result, but to me, at least they had their souls and their dignity. There were fewer souls and less dignity in Belfast, where there was so much corruption and indeed violence at that time.

Donegal was so beautiful. Yet it had its fair share of trouble from the profiteers, who were heavily involved in tourism and its related industries. Despite that, I would love to have grown up in Donegal with their sweet accents and beautiful landscapes.

It was a place set apart not only by the border between the Republic and Northern Ireland but by the difference in its ways.

I thought of the Great Famine in the 1840's and of how it had affected this beautiful county as much as any part of the country, if not more. The people had starved to death then, not on some whim as a protest against the wearing of certain types of clothes, but because there was nothing to eat.

The poverty was so great that when the potato crop failed time and again, there simply was no food to be found. There were people with their mouths turned green as they ate the very grass that grew on the sides of roads and in fields. That was a real hunger strike. Hunger had struck like never before and people, tens of thousands of them, had died because there was no food to be had.

The then British government had enforced Tory economic policies, and used their supply and demand market economy arguments to deny the Irish people the very food, especially for the elderly and children, that might have saved their lives.

Donegal was badly hit by the Great Famine. Many had made their way to Derry and other ports in order to get the boat to America. But thousands of Donegal people had died because they were unable to find the money for the boat, or indeed for some sustaining food.

It was a tragedy of massive proportions, a tragedy that had been emulated by Irish republicans in the course of their protests against the British crown throughout the twentieth century. But their protests were hollow in comparison to the impact of the famine, which left a million dead, and at least another million on the emigration ships.

It was a great moment of tragedy for Ireland, and a moment of shame for the British government. To emulate it, even in a small way, as Irish republicans had done, was to betray the memory of these beautiful people. These people didn't sacrifice themselves. They did everything to attempt to put food on their tables. There was no hollow cynicism, or protest at things done in the past, involved in their actions. They died because they were poor.

The IRA hunger strikers had died through their own choice in some senses. Equally well, it could be argued that they had had no choice since their sense of reality had left them before they embarked on their course of action. But they chose to begin their protest against their unfair treatment in a British prison, and that was utter folly. It led eventually, via the path of the dehumanising dirty protests and blanket protests, to the hunger strikes.

Most people were sympathetic to their plight. Most people wanted them to succeed, but many also accepted that they were up against the same British government who had let Donegal people die decades before, with their high "principles". The same arrogance was shown to a group of men who needed compassion, and a way out, as was shown to the people of Ireland during the Great Famine.

It was the same British government alright, who defended their lack of humanity with hollow arguments and claims to principle that were in fact just the same self-interested rhetoric of the British imperialist and capitalist tradition. There was nothing noble about the British Tory party. Theirs was a selfish, arrogant caste.

That's where the folly of the republicans lay. They expected better from the British government than the British could deliver. It was mind-boggling stupidity. The British treated the hunger strikers as they had treated the Irish for centuries - with disdain. It was tricky for the British, I'll give the hunger strikers that, due to the pressures from Irish-America, but it was right up their street.

The British were always going to be prepared to let these ten Irishmen starve themselves to death. The hunger strikers were doomed to die. The British wouldn't be capable of understanding the emotional backlash from their deaths, and thus they wouldn't understand what they were doing to Ireland.

I knew. At least I knew for certain now, as I drove towards the west coast of Ireland. Millions of pounds of funds had been sent to Ireland, and perhaps I was only seeing the tip of the ice-burg. Funds had been sent in order to fund a campaign of more bombings and death. Death begets death, not life. Jesus' resurrection begot eternal life, just as the hunger strikers' death had brought eternal death for republicans.

I arrived in the little town of Burtonport, on the western tip of the county, and parked my car at the central car park. There were a few people around on that Sunday afternoon.

I walked across the car park to the pier where a few large fishing boats had been moored. It was a haunting site. Beside my car there was a memorial to fishermen who had died in an accident at sea.

The boats did not look like hospitable places. They were cramped and I could imagine that, as the sea bounced off the sides of these small ships, it would scare any normal person off fishing for the rest of their lives.

But these fishermen were no ordinary mortals. The sea was their life, and they had become accustomed to it in a way that I could not really understand. It was their livelihood and yet it seemed such a dangerous way to make a living.

The irony struck me as I thought that. These fishermen had the elements to battle against and any fatalities at sea would usually be caused by the power of nature. Yet I was working in what was considered a very safe occupation in a city, and I was probably more likely to die than they were.

First there was the violence of cities. I could be robbed at knifepoint in the street, and my throat cut for my wallet. I could be burgled and killed by some armed burglar who I had interrupted as he went through my possessions. I could be killed in a road accident as I rushed to an appointment.

The city was as dangerous as nature, if not more dangerous. On top of the normal risks I had big Tom Brennan's investigation to deal with. The IRA seemed to want to hound me about that. I was at risk, even if it hadn't properly registered with me.

The IRA would undoubtedly kill me if I crossed them. I had no doubt about that. If their member went down for tax fraud, I might be alright. If he went down for membership, then I would go down with him. That was true even if I did nothing, not that that was really an option.

It was a frightening thought. If someone accidentally revealed that big Tom Brennan was an IRA man, and he was caught, and the tax investigation was uncovered by the RUC Special Branch, then I would be in grave danger.

Danger was the theme in my mind as I witnessed these massive boats, massive for a small port anyway, tied up along the pier. I felt strangely attracted to the boats. One in particular caught my eye. It was designed to take people over to the island of Aranmore, off the Donegal coast.

It was leaving in a half an hour according to the captain. I decided that I would go over and come back later in the afternoon. The only problem was that I couldn't take my car. The boat was not really a ferry. It could take cars, but usually only if they were being taken for use on the island on a permanent basis.

I decided that I would be better off without a car. In any case, I had been to the island before, and all the main amenities were concentrated around the pier at the other end of the voyage.

The water was choppy once we got a little way out to sea, but the boat was pretty sturdy. There were some beautiful sights to be had from the side of the ship. There was the sight of the Donegal coastline as it emerged, and there was the beauty of the little island of Aranmore as it came into sight.

The west of Ireland was indeed very special. There was almost a mysticism associated with the island. It was so peaceful looking, but it had quite a few inhabitants too. It was a paradox in the middle of the Atlantic ocean. By all logic, it shouldn't have had any inhabitants such were the inconveniences of getting there for human beings.

But it was home to some one thousand people. They were stalwarts of the natural world, who lived in one of the most natural settings in western Europe. Yet nature was a bitch when it came down to it. It began to rain heavily as soon as I disembarked from the boat and the wind was fierce.

I was going back on the next boat, I decided.

Chapter Twelve

On the island people were scurrying here and there, getting themselves under cover from the storm that was brewing. I thought I had seen the worst of the storm as I disembarked from the ferry after the short journey from mainland Ireland.

But I was quickly told that it was going to be a big storm, and that I would be better making my way to a pub or café to sit it out. I was still confident that I would be going back to the mainland after the storm on one of the returning voyages of the ferry.

But I was wrong as it turned out. I sat and drank a coffee in the only café on the island, which was situated just yards from the ferry terminal, or "the pier" as they called it locally. I could see the Atlantic Ocean being stirred up by the storm.

The sea was battering the pier with such ferocity that I felt uncomfortable being so near to the end of the pier. It had been relatively calm as we crossed the straight from Burtonport to Aranmore. There was no sign that it was going to get worse.

Nonetheless, the locals knew it would get worse. They had been having that kind of weather since before they could remember. It was natural and it was their reality.

I felt a strange attraction to the island when I realised that they had such changeable weather patterns. For all the progress man had made with technology and science, it still could not deal with nature. The storms remained a dominant feature of the world that these people lived in.

Soon I was joined at my table by a young man, who had made his way from the other end of the village surrounding the pier. I saw him coming as I had watched him get a soaking as he pushed his way against the rain.

'How are you?' he asked, as he sat on the only seat available in the small café.

'A bit worried,' I replied. The young man was not local, but he was Irish.

'Why's that now?' he asked. 'Is it the storm?'

'Yeah,' I said. 'It's getting pretty rough out there.' I nodded in the direction of the sea to emphasise my point.

'That's what the locals call a little one,' he said. 'Sure it's hardly that bad.'

'I don't want to be stuck over here,' I said.

'The island not good enough for you?' he wondered brusquely.

'No,' I said defensively, 'it's not that. I only came over for a day trip.'

He laughed. I wondered why he was laughing. I felt such a fool. Was I really stuck over here for much longer than I had anticipated?

'What's the joke?' I asked.

'Sorry,' he replied. 'I remember myself in that position last summer. I was stuck here for a week, but I decided to stay a bit longer as you see.'

'But the weather couldn't have been that bad in the summer,' I pointed out.

'No,' he said. 'The ferry broke down. It needed fixing. They had to bring parts from Cork.'

'Oh,' I said, a little more sure about the man's story. 'Why'd you stay?'

'I loved the place,' he said. 'I fell in love with the island, and with Brigid McPartland.'

I was enthralled by his revelation. He had fallen in love with a local.

He continued. 'But it's different in the summer. The sun is shining and there are many tourists around. It's a proper little busy spot. You can have a grand time here.'

'And the winter?' I asked, expecting him to tell me the obvious.

'Everyone's gone,' he replied. 'The tourists don't come. The young people are at college or school on the mainland, as they

call it here, and the weather is so desperate.'
'Why do you stay?' I asked.
'Brigid,' he said. 'The love of my life. Though I'm thinking of going as soon as the work has dried up.'
'What work is that?' I wondered, my accountancy instincts working overtime.
'Bar work,' he replied. 'I get a few shifts in the village here and at the hotel up the road.' He seemed sad to say that he worked as a barman. I realised that he was an intelligent man, and that he had an education.
'Where are you from?' I asked.
'South Armagh,' he replied, scaring the shit out of me, momentarily. I hoped he wasn't an IRA man.
'And what did you do there?' I wondered, regaining my composure.
'Oh, I had just graduated from UCD,' he said. I laughed.
'I'm a UCG man myself,' I said, extending my hand to shake his. 'My name is John,' I added.
'Kieran,' he said. 'Kieran McGreevy.' He smiled at me, revealing a charming face under the cap he was wearing. 'I graduated in Law and French.'
'Jesus,' I said, 'you should be working in Dublin or Brussels, not Aranmore.'
Kieran tipped his head back and wiped his forehead of the remnants of the rain, and sighed.
'That's what my parents say,' he said eventually. 'They have it all mapped out for me. I thought that I would go down that path too, but I don't want to do it just to please my parents. They have a building firm, you see. And they want the best for me, their only son. I know they feel that it's best for me.'
'But you don't?' I wondered.
'Not now,' he replied, almost in a whisper. 'Now I feel that I've found my soul, and I want this little island to be my home for ever more. Only I know it won't last. The feeling, I mean.'

'Why not?' I wondered.

'It won't last because I can't fucking stand the weather in the winters,' he said. 'It's great in the summer. It's like a mild winter sometimes, but it's great. The winters are extreme, like today. You get soaked everywhere you go. It's not on.'

'But it's nature,' I said.

'Yeah,' Kieran said as he looked over my shoulder at the rain coming down and the boats bouncing up and down in the sea beside the pier. I looked too and I could understand what he meant. He didn't need to say anything. It was nature alright. Who could blame him for wanting to be somewhere else?

'You'll have to book in tonight,' he said.

'What?' I asked.

'That's on for the night,' he explained. 'The boat'll stay here overnight, and there might be a sailing tomorrow.'

'Where do I stay?'

'In the hotel, of course,' Kieran said. 'I'll take you up there later. I'm working there this evening.'

Kieran sat quietly and ate his apple square as I looked out onto the stormy sea beyond the pier. The ferryboat was being moored as if it had no intention of leaving the island for a fairly long time. It was probably being tied up to avoid any damage being done to it during the storm, which seemed to be ever more ferocious.

It was a terrifying scenario for me. I had rarely seen the weather change so quickly and so extremely in such a short period of time. It was the way of the islands off the coast of Ireland, and especially off the coast of Donegal.

I wondered what Brigid was like. Kieran seemed to love her in a very intense way so I thought that she must have been a very attractive girl. Kieran was a handsome man in his own way, and I was sure that he would have picked the belle of the ball.

When Kieran had finished he got up, and bade me to rise with him.

'I'll take you up there now if you want?' he said, pointing to the hill beside the pier. 'The rain's eased off, so we'll need to be moving.'

I got up, and walked to the door. I noticed the captain of the ferry, coming into the café and I asked him about the crossings.

'There'll be none till the morning,' he said with his Donegal tone. 'I'm very sorry.'

The wind blew fiercely in our faces as we made our way up the steep slope to the hotel. I thought a few times about stopping, or going back, but it seemed best just to stay behind Kieran.

The hotel was a modest affair. It was small, with perhaps less than twenty bedrooms, but it had a large dancing area in the centre of the lounge, no doubt where the locals came for their weekend entertainment.

I went directly to reception on entering the hotel. I wanted to get to my room so that I could dry off after the lashing we took on the way up to the building, when the rain had come down in buckets.

'Where's the receptionist?' I asked Kieran, as he moved behind the counter. Kieran smiled.

'Here I am,' he said. 'My shift's just started.'

'I thought you did the bar,' I said.

'I do almost everything,' Kieran laughed.

'Good,' I said. 'You can get me a good room at the right price.'

'Small, medium, or large price?' Kieran asked.

'Medium, I suppose,' I replied.

We agreed a price of IR£30 and I took myself to my room, which was just down the corridor on the left. It was a nice room. The bed was firm and the sheets were dazzlingly clean.

From the window I could see over the village and out into the Atlantic, which we had crossed earlier that day.

It was an amazing scene. The waves had got very large, and I could almost see the angry white "horses" bash into the pier.

There was a boat out at sea, and it seemed to be trying to make its way to shore. I feared for its occupants, as it was being pushed about like a toy boat in a wild child's bath. I telephoned reception to tell Kieran about it. I wanted to be sure that the lifeboats had been launched.

Kieran already knew about the boat, and had made enquiries. The lifeboat, he said, wouldn't go out on a day like that, but the helicopter had been launched from Bundoran, just down the coast, and was on its way. He said there were three people on the boat, but that they were all experienced fishermen, and they would be all right.

I watched from the window to see if the helicopter would arrive. It did after ten minutes. It hovered above the boat, and communicated with the crew, who had probably made an S.O.S. call.

A crewman from the helicopter was winched down to the boat, which rose up and down wildly on the waves. It seemed that one of the fishermen was injured since the crewman pulled out a stretcher and they seemed to work for ages to get this man on board. Eventually he was winched up and to the safety of the helicopter.

The helicopter disappeared after that, and the two remaining fishermen made their way to the shore in a very haphazard way that saw their boat cross and criss-cross the front of the beach. They were very lucky to get there, I thought. Then again, they were very experienced fishermen, and undoubtedly there was more to it than luck.

I lay down after that, taking my trousers off and letting them dry over the heater. I fell asleep eventually. It was a tiring day.

I had been through much and I felt relieved to be resting.

I woke about an hour later, the noise of the storm beating at the window having broken my sleep. Darkness was falling, and the storm seemed to be getting even more ferocious.

I put on my trousers, which were by now dry, and my shoes. I went to the hotel bar where Kieran was sitting with a few people.

'This is John, Brigid,' he said on seeing me.

'How are you?' Brigid said. 'I'm the owner of the hotel, and Kieran is my partner as he told you.' She laughed: 'My *current* partner, I'll have him know.'

I stood aghast for an instant. Brigid was the owner. That meant both her and Kieran were likely to be staying in the hotel.

'Nice to meet you,' I said. I didn't know whether or not it was nice since Brigid seemed to be quite a few years older than Kieran. His mother would be furious. It was little wonder that his parents wanted him to continue with his career in law.

'You're not getting the weather you expected,' Brigid said, grinning. She was a woman in her late thirties, who had obviously been around a fair bit. She knew how to handle a guest, and she knew how to charm a man.

'You're not joking,' I said. I looked at her with her beautiful, sincere Donegal smile. She was a very attractive woman, who had obviously charmed poor little Kieran into staying with her after a summer romance.

'I suppose you'd want something to eat,' Kieran said. The Armagh man seemed proud of his Donegal catch. He seemed very happy that he was only seeing the belle of Aranmore, the hotel owner herself.

'I would,' I said. 'I'm starving.'

'There's a menu over there,' he said. 'Pick what you like and give us a shout. We'll have it cooked up in no time.'

I went over and sat with the menu for a few moments. There were a lot of fish dishes, as well as the usual steaks and such like. I went for a cod dish since it was bound to be the most fresh in this little fishing area.

Kieran took the order to the kitchen, and it seemed that he was going to cook it himself until he returned moments later with the news that the cook was "a bit late" and that he would be there soon.

'I'll deduct it from his wages,' Brigid said, grinning again, as if she really knew who was boss. She turned to me then.

'Kieran says that you wanted to go back this evening,' she said.

'Yeah,' I said. 'I was only over to rekindle some old memories. You see, I came over here a few times as a teenager about a decade ago, and we had camped on the edge of the beach.'

'That was in the summer?' Brigid wondered.

'Well,' I said, 'we came here at Easter one year, but we were frozen out of it by bad weather.'

'A bit like now,' she said.

'Yeah.'

We got into conversation about the rescue out at sea that afternoon and Brigid told me that the fisherman had almost lost his arm in an accident on the boat, and that he was lucky to be alive.

On hearing the story, I wasn't looking forward to the journey home the next day. If the weather changed again, we might be stranded or drowned in those raging waters of the north Atlantic.

It was an unappetising thought.

The meal was very appetising when it came about an hour later, by which time I had downed a couple of pints of beer.

Brigid and Kieran were good company, and there were plenty of laughs. They seemed like the perfect couple despite their age difference, which meant that Brigid was almost old enough to be Kieran's mother. Brigid left to check the rooms at one point, and I jibed Kieran a bit about his relationship.

'You fell on your feet here,' I said.

'Oh yeah,' he said. 'I really love her. She's a delight.'

'She likes the younger man, I see,' I added. Kieran laughed.

'Yes,' he said, 'and I like the older woman.'

'Is it a mother thing?' I wondered, trying to be an amateur psychologist.

'Fuck off,' Kieran laughed. 'She's like a mother in some ways, but she is a very sexy lady.'

'I'll bet,' I laughed. 'You're a lucky bloke. You wouldn't get many like her in south Armagh.'

'No,' he said. 'It's strange, isn't it? I go all the way to Aranmore Island in west Donegal, where everyone is supposed to be so Catholic and conservative, and I find love in a usually forbidden relationship with an older woman.'

'It's strange, yeah,' I smiled.

'If I'd have gone to London or New York with my classmates, I'd have probably met a stuffy oul' nun, if you know what I mean,' he added. Kieran seemed so content with himself and with Brigid.

To me, it was a bit risqué for him to get so deep into a relationship with an older woman in such circumstances. She could have been using him for the sex. He was young and good-looking, and she could have even convinced herself that he was the right man for her. She might waken up some morning and realise that she was not really in love with him.

Kieran would be hurt then and it would be disastrous for him. In the place where he had gone to nourish his soul, he would leave with his self-respect and even his dignity in tatters. The one sure thing about someone with Brigid's disposition, owning as she did a hotel and also a bar, which Kieran told me about, in a small island, was that she would call the shots.

Then I chatted with Brigid, Kieran having gone to do something in the hotel basement.

Brigid was a farmer's daughter from west Donegal, who had sold the land on her father's death to tourism developers and invested it in the hotel, then the bar, on the island. It wasn't far from home, but she had no ties on the island.

The locals were very shy with her at first, not really accepting her, until she had "served her apprenticeship" of several years on the island. After that "rite of passage" they became more certain about her. She had been on the island for seven years.

She liked Kieran. He was a little naïve, but he was good fun to be with. It seemed that Kieran was good for the sexual side of their relationship.

'I know you may think that I might hurt him,' she admitted, 'but I won't. If need be, I'll let him down gently. I've been hurt a few times in recent years, and I would never wish it on anyone.'

'Sure, how would anyone hurt you?' I mused.

'Well, John,' she said, 'there's this damn hotel for a start. Everyone thinks I'm here for the taking, a ripe old lady with a fortune under my mattress. All the young bucks want a go at me, and they don't usually stop until they've drawn blood, if you know what I mean. They get their claws in, and they want everything. And when I can't give it, they try to destroy me.'

'That's sad,' I said. As I listened to her, I could detect that Brigid was a sincere enough woman. 'You know,' I said, 'it seems that this place is no different from Belfast where I work. There are lots of sharks there too.'

'Don't talk to me about sharks,' Brigid laughed wryly. 'I've seen more sharks on this island than in the ocean that surrounds it.'

I felt sad at that. It was a tragedy to think that this beautiful island could not offer a better way of life than the cities. It was appalling to think that there were people who would use and abuse other people as if they had some divine right to interfere where they weren't wanted.

The island was modernising. I could detect in the accents that the age of innocence was on its way to being lost. Yet I could also detect that the innocence was not yet lost. Brigid would have had a hell of a time in a place like Belfast. She wouldn't have known what hit her.

The loss of innocence was much more apparent in Belfast. There was violence there too, and sectarian differences that, throughout the course of our conversation, Brigid could never manage to understand. I found it difficult to understand myself.

No-one could understand hatred unless they saw it at first hand. No-one could know bigotry unless they had experienced it, perhaps only then by being on the wrong end of it. Sure, Brigid knew all the words and the slogans, but she didn't understand how anyone could kill for those same slogans.

I sort of knew. I could sense it in the passion and the anger of my Nationalist friends. But I could never understand it fully.

This was a heartening thought. I knew I was among good people because they didn't really understand the motivations of people who existed at the raw ends of the killing machines in the republican and loyalist communities.

I could sense, too, that Brigid would not have killed over anything or for anything. She was her own woman, doing very well in life. She seemed happy, even if she was dating a man who was much younger than her. She seemed content despite having to fight off the "young bucks" who were just interested in her wealth.

Brigid was a tragic figure too in a sense. She was in reality alone at the age of thirty-eight. She had Kieran, sure, but he was going to leave soon enough, and she would have to find someone else to keep her warm at night.

Her husband had died, she said, soon after their wedding in a road traffic accident. Another tragedy had brought her to Aranmore, her father having died to leave her a farm with development potential.

It seemed at face value that she had everything she wanted, but it was more true to say that she had everything once and then lost it along the way. She was going to lose Kieran eventually, and that would really hurt her more than him.

As I sat there talking to Brigid and Kieran, I was overcome with love for these two people, who had swam against the tide in modern European terms, and had landed themselves on a beautiful island surrounded by mainly beautiful, honest people.

Some of the young men might have wanted Brigid's money, but that was, I detected, part of the romance of the island for her. It was good to be wanted.

I could understand more about big Tom Brennan as I sat in the lounge overlooking the village and the beach of Aranmore. I could understand the romance of his money, even if it wasn't really his. I could understand the emptiness in people like him that sometimes needs to be filled with little, or big, sums of money and wealth.

But I couldn't work out where his desire to have a cause fitted in. Brigid had no cause that I could detect. She wasn't on the island because she wanted to protect the falling population from extinction. She wasn't there to provide a charitable service, going by the prices in the hotel anyway, or to help the natives.

She was there because she wanted a business, and it was probably the only one available within her price range. She would possibly leave to go somewhere else in a few years, having made enough money to secure the purchase of another Donegal hotel.

On the other hand, big Tom Brennan was going through a lean period in terms of his dignity. He had been caught by the

British authorities, the very authorities he was fighting in Ireland, and it must have rankled. He may not have even been to blame in the final analysis.

He may have been advised that IRA sympathisers in the offshore banks were taking care of the money and that there was no need to be too careful. After all, he had got away with it for nearly a decade when he was caught.

Nonetheless, caught he was. Red-handed, looking as stupid as can be. He was sitting with around two million pounds, and not the slightest chance of finding a reason for having produced £500,000 in excess undeclared profit in a single year.

By all reason, he should have been quaking in his boots. He should have been looking forward to a fairly lengthy stretch as a guest of Her Majesty, the very Queen he was fighting with the money in the first place. He should have been looking at three to five years in prison.

If Special Branch got hold of his file, he would have been looking at maybe a ten year stretch; longer if they could find anything else on him when they delved deeper into his activities and background.

He was cool for a man in that predicament. Maybe it was to do with the fact that he had a cause, and he felt that he was right in what he was doing, and no matter what the British threw at him, he would suffer it as so many like him had suffered it over the decades of the Troubles.

Brigid and Kieran had a cause only in the sense that their cause was each other. Love was their cause, and they pursued it with jealous dedication and a perseverance that can only come from the knowledge that it might not last forever.

Strangely I thought that their love would last forever, but strangely also, I thought that they would not always be together. Their love was a paradox, like love was, sometimes.

I went to bed in the hotel that night, sure in the knowledge that however much I was stuck on the island, there was little chance that the IRA would be able to get over to me and harass me.

It was an amusing thought. They couldn't get me now, even if they wanted to. There were no warnings that I was not to talk to "the wrong person". There were no incidents of aggression from IRA members, or subterfuge from the renegade Knights of Columbanus.

I was safe on the island.

Chapter Thirteen

I woke early on Monday morning with the sound of gulls outside my window. For a moment I was unsure where I was, the new surrounds a little confusing to my emerging consciousness. Then I realised I was on the island.

'Fucking great,' I whispered. 'Nobody can get to me out here.'

Then the realisation came that I might be going back to the mainland that morning if the ferry was able to cross the straight. It was a disturbing thought. I had had something of a little retreat on the island the day before, when all my worries had kind of disappeared.

Of course, they hadn't completely disappeared. Not in one day. Not ever, I thought. They were the kind of problems that needed to be addressed, not avoided. But I needed the mental energy and the insight to arrive at a solution to them.

I looked out the window, after I had struggled out of bed, my head slightly sore after the drinking of the previous night. The sea still seemed to be at war with the island. The waves raced into the shore with such a velocity that it seemed that they were being caused by underwater earthquakes.

'Brilliant,' I whispered. 'They'll not be crossing today.'

I thought that even if there was a crossing, I would be inclined to stay a few days just to experience life on the island. I had said as much to Kieran in a drink-induced haze the previous night. But I recalled that he had warned me that I would be best getting across while I could, or I might face a week or so on the island.

It had been known for the island to be cut off from the mainland for weeks, and for Irish army helicopters to have to land food and supplies on the island. It was not a pleasant time since there were shortages of all the luxuries that made living on the island tolerable for people like Brigid.

So if there was a crossing that day, I would most likely be on it. It was a depressing thought. I wanted to go back to bed and dream a little more about being on the island. It had become such a part of me. I had only been on the island for one day and now it seemed as if I needed it more than anything.

I walked to the bathroom, shaved and washed my face. Then I had a shower. Water and electricity were in good supply at least, I thought. It was a beautiful warm shower.

I got dressed and went out to the lounge to see if anyone was around. The clock said it was nine o'clock. I expected everyone to be up.

Only Kieran was up. He was washing the floor of the lounge with a mop when I disturbed him.

'Sore head?' he asked.

'Not too bad now,' I replied. 'I've had a shower.'

'You should have lain in,' he said. 'There's nothing happening around here this early.'

'What about the ferry?' I wondered.

'Look out the window,' he said. 'It'll not be leaving here this morning.'

'What about this afternoon?' I enquired.

'I don't know,' he said. 'There might be a break in the storm in a few hours, but not this morning.'

I poured myself a glass of water and sat down at the window overlooking the village and the beach. It was a scary sight to see the sea so angry and aggressive. But it was possibly even more scary if the sea had been calm and I had to go back to the mainland.

Kieran sat with me after a while, telling me that he would cook up a breakfast when he had a chance to rest his feet for a minute. Brigid and he took turns to get up early and do the work.

'So what do you think of the hotel?' Kieran asked as he sat beside me at the window.

I knew that it was a loaded question. He was really asking me what I thought about his home and his life with Brigid.

'Excellent,' I said discreetly. 'You couldn't beat this sort of life.'

'I'm glad you like it,' he said. 'I'm very attached to it myself. I don't know what I would do without Brigid.'

As soon as he mentioned Brigid, I knew that he was asking me about their relationship and their living together while unmarried on the island.

'She's a lovely woman,' I said.

'She is,' he said firmly. 'She's the best.'

There was silence for a moment, as I couldn't think of anything to say. Brigid *was* a lovely woman. She was a very attractive woman, and good-natured too. She was the kind of woman I would marry if I had a chance. Then Kieran, as if reading my mind, mentioned marriage.

'We're happy as things are,' he said. 'Getting married might only cause controversy here on the island and affect her business with the locals.'

'I didn't mean to imply that you should marry her,' I hurriedly said. 'Brigid's lovely, but you have to decide about those things on your own.'

'I know,' Kieran said solemnly. 'I didn't mean to infer that you did. But I would love us to get married. There's only the age difference. What do you think? You're a Northerner, and this is a Northerner thing.'

'How do you mean?' I asked, startled.

'We're different up there,' he said. 'We have so much to run away from. Sometimes we don't know what we're running from. Sometimes it's the Troubles.'

'I suppose,' I agreed, impressed by his wisdom. 'And you're worried that your feelings for Brigid are so strong because you're running away from something?'

'Yes.'

'Give it time,' I said. 'Don't rush into anything. You'll find out who you are soon enough. You're really just out of school for the first time in your life. I felt that the world was at my feet when I came out of university and soon found that I was at the feet of the world, if you know what I mean.'

'At the bottom of the heap, you mean,' Kieran added.

'Yeah.'

'Well, I'm on top of the world now,' Kieran said. 'It's just that it's a small world, a tiny island, and I'm not sure that I'm living an escape.'

'We're all living an escape in one way or other,' I said. 'It's the same for me in the city. We're all not facing reality. All of us find reality a difficult thing to face up to.'

Kieran paused for a moment as he absorbed my words. I was kicking myself for stating what were honest words, since I could almost guess his next question.

'What are you running away from?' he asked, not disappointing me.

'I…,' I stammered. 'I'm…'

'You don't want to talk about it,' he said. 'That's all right. You're with friends here.'

'I'm dealing with a difficult situation at work,' I said finally. 'But you're right. I don't want to talk about it. It's very complex.'

He was dead right. I didn't want to talk to him about it. Not to him at any rate. I couldn't talk to a south Armagh Catholic about my problem with the IRA. He might be straight on the phone and soon I'd be swarmed with threats and intimidation.

Nonetheless, Kieran was different. He was a wise head on young shoulders. He wouldn't be a typical IRA supporter if he were one. But south Armagh was a tight-knit community and everyone was bound to know someone who knew an IRA member. It wouldn't be wise to get into the detail of my problems with Kieran.

Kieran rose, half-embarrassed, to make the breakfast. I was starving, my stomach rumbling from the beer the night before, and so I was glad to see him move to the kitchen.

It was a beautiful breakfast by any standards. It began with a cereal and orange juice. Then eggs, sausages and bacon were heaped on my plate as well as beans, fried mushrooms and tomato. It was all washed down with a beautiful pot of tea. I was very content.

Then I realised that I was on my own, and upon enquiring, Kieran told me that I was the only guest. All the others in the hotel the night before, who had stayed up longer than me, were locals enjoying the creature comforts in their local hostelry.

It was strange being the only guest in a hotel. It felt weird. Yet it made me feel secure in the knowledge that I wasn't being watched or followed. Kieran told me that there were others stranded on the island but they had gone to the Bed and Breakfast houses along the shore front, which were cheaper, or to the homes of relatives.

Brigid arrived from her room eventually. She was tired looking, despite her lie-in. She was cheerful enough to me, of course, but I could tell that she was having some bother. She told me that she felt a cold coming on, and ribbed Kieran about pulling the duvet off her during the night.

Eventually she went out to do some shopping in the local general store, and left me alone with Kieran. We watched her drive her jeep down the hill the short distance to the shop in the village.

Kieran switched on the radio, and it struck me immediately that we hadn't watched any television the night before. I was happy at that. Television was such a pain in the ass, and it was much better just to sit around and talk. The lack of a television was something that I recalled from my student days in Galway, when we had no television most of the time, and we really didn't miss it.

Then, of course, the news came on the radio. It was the RTE news and the headline was that four British soldiers had been blown up in a bombing near the border in south Armagh.

'Fucking magic,' Kieran roared, punching his fist in the air.

I grinned and bore his joy, but I was most perturbed. Those soldiers had families too, and I wanted to tell Kieran to shut up and think about someone else for a change. But he noticed that I wasn't so keen on the news.

'You're not into the Provos,' he said. 'I can tell.'

'Not really,' I said. 'I'm against violence.'

'I'm sorry,' Kieran said. 'I just assumed that any Northerner who came this far into the most Gaelic part of Ireland must be a republican.'

'I'm not,' I said. 'I love Ireland, but I hate violence.'

'Actually,' he said. 'I don't like the Provos that much either, but when it comes to British soldiers, I just get carried away. I think they're bastards who shouldn't be there.'

'The deaths of British soldiers don't bother me much either,' I said. 'But I don't get overjoyed at it. They have families who suffer because of our dirty little sectarian conflict. But you're right, they shouldn't be there.'

'Brigid is very moderate,' Kieran revealed. 'She's totally against the IRA. But she's a Free-Stater, and they don't know any better. They don't know what we go through up there.'

The room fell silent after that. What did we go through up there in Kieran's mind? He was a Law and French graduate from a middleclass family in south Armagh. The war had probably rarely even touched his entire family circle never mind him. He was revealing a different side to his character.

The good-natured, wise young man that I had known him as had all but disappeared, and he was showing an angrier side to his character. That was the effect the North had on young people. The idealism they learned at school soon became replaced by an anger that the world was not what they expected.

If only he knew that the war was directed by gangsters, and there was no room in their plans for gentle minds like his.

Then again, why did he presume that an accountant like me would support the IRA? Was he revealing a knowledge of south Armagh republicans that deduced that there were business and professional people at the centre of their organisation, or even just on the periphery?

It was strange that he had assumed that I would cheer because British soldiers had died. In actual fact, a part of me was always enthralled at attacks on the British army. It probably went back to my understanding of Irish history and an intuitive feeling that we were winning when the British army was having a bad time.

I couldn't see how we were winning now. The British Exchequer were taking two million pounds of IRA money and lodging it in the current account for expenditure on troops and fortresses across the North.

But I admired Kieran's honesty. It was naïve in a sense, but it was at least honest. No-one liked British soldiers. I didn't like them, even though they were mostly courteous to me at checkpoints and on the occasions that they passed me in the street. They were caught in the middle between two warring tribes in some senses.

In another sense they had no right to be there, and their presence was antagonistic to many people in my own community. Their historic right to be in Ireland had dubious credibility, and the British government had simply used the soldiers to repress "the natives" in historic terms.

Nonetheless, there was a humanitarian aspect to their presence. These were the sons and daughters of the British working class. They were in Ireland fighting to separate parts of the Irish working class, both Protestant and Catholic. A lot of people were dying in this conflict, and they were mainly working class people.

They were dying because some people wanted to fight for such concepts as "the right of the Irish people to national self-determination", and "the right to majority rule in Northern Ireland". These were luxuries which ordinary people rarely understood, and never really benefited from. These were the policies of establishments, and not the politics of ordinary people. So in a sense all violence did was to leave victims to wonder why their loved ones had died.

In a sense too, something that really stuck in my craw was the fact these people in paramilitary organisations always talked about representing the working class. I knew from my own roots in the communities of Derry, where I was brought up among the working class, albeit in a well-off family in a comparable sense, having both parents working, that the working class were by and large against violence.

It was a slander on the working class to assume that the republicans were fighting a war on behalf of the working class. Class, in my opinion, was not an issue. The ordinary families of Derry were as much against war as the middleclass families. More so, sometimes, to the extent that they involved themselves in political organisations, such as the SDLP, to send out a very firm rejection of violence.

The real war was not between working class communities. It was between middle class business and professional people, who had managed to convince elements of the working class to become cannon fodder for the cause. These uncouth members of the working class let their class down when they fought under the direction of the professional class.

The real war was between businessmen.

Chapter Fourteen

'So this is the west coast,' I declared to a charming Brigid, who had volunteered to give me a tour of the island in her jeep. 'It's absolutely beautiful.'

'Isn't it just,' Brigid said loudly. 'We don't come out here enough.'

Kieran had decided to man the hotel bar while Brigid showed me some of the sights of the island. It was a really beautiful island. There was no doubt about that. There were lots of little cottages and bungalows, dotted on the edges of the road, where the bulk of the people of the island lived.

The road ran in a circle around the outskirts of the island. I imagined that it would be a beautiful experience in summer to walk the whole distance, a matter of a couple of miles. It wouldn't be so enjoyable in winter when the rain and wind, together with the cold, would "cut you in half".

We saw the occasional islander walking by on the roadside, possibly going to a neighbour's house, but they were few and far between. Nothing would have enticed me out of the jeep on a day like that. The wind was cutting and the rain, though sporadic, would have soaked you to the skin in an instant.

'It's a lazy wind today,' Brigid said. I was confused by what she meant as I felt that there was nothing but extreme energy in the wind.

'What do you mean?' I asked.

'Oh,' she laughed, 'it's an old saying. It means that the wind doesn't take time to go around you. It goes straight through you. It's very cutting in other words.'

I laughed. It was an entirely appropriate saying in the circumstances. It was indeed a "lazy wind".

Brigid stopped at a bungalow to say "hello" to a friend. She invited me in. A young woman appeared at the door. She was very attractive, and I greeted her as she closed the door tightly behind me.

'Who's the handsome man?' she asked Brigid.

'He's staying with us for a time,' Brigid said discreetly. 'His name is John.' Brigid then introduced me to her friend, who was called Carole-Anne. She looked around next and asked about the woman's mother. 'Where's Josie today?'

'Mammy's in bed with a flu,' Carole-Anne said.

'Do you need anything in?' Brigid asked.

'No,' Carole-Anne said, 'we're fine for the moment.'

As the women talked I sat back in admiration at the nature of their community on the island. They looked out for each other. They took care of each other, and they really were at ease with one another.

It was a perfect Christian island in the midst of a world where Christianity was being forgotten or defined as simply and purely about sexual morality.

Carole-Anne made us the most beautiful cup of tea I had tasted in a long time, and it was only afterwards, when I asked Brigid about it, that I found out that there was a little taste of poteen in the brew "just to flavour it".

It was the one thing that I had noticed about the island. There was no police presence. The nearest Garda station was on the mainland, which meant that there was a lax attitude to law and order. Not only was poteen available, but it was possibly the best poteen in the country since there were no worries about being caught during the brewing process.

I liked Carole-Anne. She was a child of the island, who had left in search of her fortune in Dublin, and had returned to nurse her elderly mother, now that she had separated from her husband. She had no children, and would have been a fine catch for any man worth his salt.

She was the salt of the earth. She told me that her husband was "a bastard", who had begun to beat her just before she left him. Apparently he had a drink problem.

I felt so calm and almost happy in her presence. The only part of me that felt sad was the part that realised that her life was tragic in some senses, from the failure of her marriage to her return as a spinster to the island.

I blamed the emergence of modern Ireland with its distinctive loss of character, and its westernisation, for the differences arising between Carole-Anne and her husband. The islanders were innocent and were always going to be completely distinctive and isolated from the mainland concerns about the liberal agenda and the advance of capitalism. What they had was community, and they had it in abundance.

I hugged Carole-Anne as I left her. She was such a lovely woman. She was a fair bit younger than Brigid, but she seemed much older than me because I was so young then. But she was a real dream.

Brigid then drove across the southern side of the island until we arrived at the Catholic Chapel. She stopped there, surprising me, since she wanted to talk to the priest.

Fr Gallagher, as he was called, was in a thoughtful mood as he dealt with Brigid's query. I could see him scratching his head as if to try to generate more brain cells to deal with the complexity of her problem.

I got out of the jeep to have a look at the chapel, remembering that the previous time I entered one, I had what I regarded as a message from the priest not to talk to "the wrong person". I didn't know whether the priest had been acting on orders from the Knights of Columbanus, and I didn't care now.

The chapel was beautiful inside, simple but beautiful. It was a fitting chapel for an island where so much was beautiful. Eventually the priest and Brigid approached me, and Brigid introduced me.

'You're a Derry man then?' Fr Gallagher asked, Brigid having told him.

'Yes,' I replied. 'From the Maiden City'

'I'm from there myself,' he said. 'It's been a while, but I was brought up there.'

'What part are you from?' I asked.

'Rosemount,' he replied. 'And you?'

'Pennyburn.'

He laughed at this. We both did. We were near neighbours from neighbouring districts, even though age was not on his side.

'Do you think that I could have a word with you in private?' I asked, after making his acquaintance and experiencing his warmth and his good-nature.

We walked to the side of the chapel, as Brigid went back to the jeep, and he asked me what was troubling me.

'I know that when men come to the island alone they're usually troubled,' he continued.

'Well,' I said, 'I have a dilemma.'

'Tell me about it, my son,' Fr Gallagher said.

I explained that I had come across a very large sum of money that belonged to the IRA and that they were threatening me and trying to intimidate me into keeping silent about it. This had led to a dilemma for me, I explained.

'Should I cower under a stone, or should I protect myself, thereby sending a man, or several men, to jail for a very long time?' I wondered.

'It's not easy to answer a question like that,' Fr Gallagher said. 'I wouldn't know what you should do. These men are dangerous. They could get at you wherever you go.

'What I would do is pray about it, and ask the question what Jesus would do about it. Don't worry if you come out with a difficult answer. I don't regard you to be cowering under a stone on this island, if that's what you think you are doing. You're actually being very brave, since many a man would have broken under the stress of such a situation.'

'Maybe I am breaking under the stress,' I postulated.

'No, you would know,' the priest said. 'You would certainly know about something like that. You seem to be handling it well.'

'But God only knows what they have in store for me,' I sighed. The priest thought for a moment, his head lowering in a pensive mode, and then looked me in the eye.

'I could telephone the Bishop of Derry for you,' he finally said. 'I might need to go through my Bishop first – you know, we're in a different diocese – but I think they would understand your dilemma.'

'That won't be necessary,' I assured him. 'But thanks for offering.' I didn't want to involve the clergy, partly because of the experience I had had with my own priest in Derry city, but mostly because I knew that it would restrict my final decision – I would be bound in many ways to take their advice. That would be an unacceptable price to pay for me. I wanted to resolve this issue in my own way, and do something that made me feel comfortable with my life again.

'I might take you up on that offer some time soon,' I said to the old priest, 'but for the moment I'm going to try to resolve the matter in my own way. They might not take kindly to me embarrassing them with the Church, and they might just deny that anything happened and leave me looking very stupid.'

'I see, my son,' Fr Gallagher said. 'Always remember to do what Jesus would do, and you will find an answer.'

We left it at that and I said my farewells to the old cleric. Brigid wanted to know what we were talking about as soon as I got into the jeep.

'Private business,' I said with a smile.

'I don't mean to pry,' Brigid said, ' but I hope you weren't talking about Kieran and me.'

'Not at all,' I said, wondering where she was coming from.

'That's good,' she said. 'We haven't told many people about

our relationship. Fr Gallagher doesn't know, and he thinks Kieran is just staff.'

'He's probably guessed,' I said. 'He's a shrewd old guy.'

'No, he doesn't know,' Brigid assured me.

We drove to the pier next where, much to my shock, the ferry was just leaving the harbour's edge. Brigid tried to halt it, by flashing her lights and sounding her horn, as we drove across the front of the island and through the village, but it continued on its way.

A fisherman at the harbour's edge told me that the captain had decided to make a journey back to the mainland at short notice, while there was a lull in the storm. The ferry was not really safe on the island and its natural moorings were in Burtonport harbour. He intended to come back if the lull continued.

I was disappointed in some senses. In another sense I was elated that I had more time to spend on the island. Nonetheless, I went back to the hotel to gather up my things and pay the bill so that I would be ready should the ferry come across again.

As I sat on my own in the lounge, I wondered about the old priest's words of advice. What would Jesus do? What would the Son of God do if he were presented with my dilemma?

It seemed at first that it was ridiculous even to attempt to get into the mind of Jesus in relation to a problem that involved money and power. Jesus would never have put himself into such a situation. He would be too clever or too good. He would never allow evil to enter his life in this way.

Yet it seemed so natural on the island to get into the way of thinking like Jesus. The islanders had a natural way of life. In many senses they faced the kind of uncertainties that the disciples of Jesus faced. They were fishermen by and large, and their families survived mainly on the fishermen's incomes.

They faced danger, and death was always on their minds as the stormy waters of the north Atlantic created the near certainty that someone would be taken sooner or later. It was a life at the edge where God was present in a very real sense. Their faith in God was all the stronger for it.

Perhaps that was why the old priest had advised me to seek Jesus's answer to my dilemma. It was the natural thing for him to suggest to an islander, since it meant something to them with their deep faith in God. To an outsider, it was less sensible advice.

Yet it was probably the best advice that a human being could get anywhere. The best answer to any dilemma was to put yourself in the position of Christ, with his complete faith in God, and seek to arrive at a conclusion.

The first thing I concluded was that Christ wouldn't think like an accountant. I had therefore to forget that I was an accountant. That wasn't going to be easy. But I tried. It took me a long time to deal with the issue of my being an accountant, but it became clear that we were called to certain professions, and accountancy was probably not one of them.

Then again, it was. I could easily acknowledge that Christ would not want us to be soldiers, or armed policemen, or even prison warders or judges, but I could not rule out accountancy as an unchristian occupation.

Someone had to pay taxes, or else there would be no government or public services, and the accountant was an essential part of that framework. The government could of course privatise accountancy and have all the accountants working for them, rather than on the side of the client.

But that didn't make sense and, unless they created a military state, where tyranny ruled, a public service accountancy would always exist to protect the client's interest in his dealings with the government.

No, accountancy wasn't the problem. It dealt only with information as presented by the client. The clients were the problem.

They had an agenda sometimes. Big Tom Brennan was a case in point. He wanted things everyway.

He wanted to be able to store money for the purpose of overthrowing the state, and yet he wanted live in that state, and take from government services. I was confused, and yet I still came to the conclusion that I should not try to think like an accountant.

When I was growing up, I hated corruption, and accountants always had a bad image as being in some way corrupt. We thought that they falsified people's accounts. This was not true in general, I found out later when I trained as one, but it was true in rare circumstances. It was always at the behest of the client that something was massaged or changed to suit their needs.

In those circumstances the accountant came into his own as knowing sufficient about the system to enable him to smuggle falsified information past the Inland Revenue. Ultimately, what I found out from the case of big Tom Brennan and my boss Sean was that accountants were complicit in corruption.

They may not have been corrupt, but they knew about corruption. They used this knowledge to protect their clients, and to advance their own reputation among clients, especially ones who were prepared to be discreet and had a lot of money to spend on accountancy fees.

My feeling was that Sean was turning a deliberate blind eye to the republican aspects of the offshore bank deposits of his client in return for massive fees.

I was beginning to see my dilemma as a layman, rather than as an accountant, but I needed time to think it through.

I dozed off after a while, the sleepy atmosphere in the hotel affecting me.

Chapter Fifteen

Carole-Anne appeared at the hotel later that evening. She was looking ravenously beautiful in a sexy red dress with her hair pushed back, revealing her strong facial characteristics and her naturally attractive, unmade-up face. She approached with purpose.

'Where's your room?' she asked bluntly, but sensuously. 'Show me around it.'

I was taken aback, but it seemed the most natural thing in the world to get up and walk towards the room, hand-in-hand with Carole-Anne.

When we got to the room, she lay on the bed, and beckoned me to lie on top of her. She was a strong woman, with strong arms and powerful shoulders, and I could see the ripples of her slender muscles on these parts of her body.

I couldn't believe my luck. She wanted me to lie on top of her. I got on the bed beside her, and looked at her in the eye. She was a very attractive woman, with strong cheekbones, and a slender chin with beautiful dimples in her cheeks.

I kissed her, as she pulled me on top of her. It was a beautiful kiss, the kind of kiss only undertaken by those who really care about each other. I hardly knew her, but I felt that I really cared about her, and her aged mother.

Carole-Anne was a beautiful kisser. I felt an unbelievable attraction to her. I just wanted to make love to her, and tell her that everything would be all right.

We made love and it was a beautiful and sensitive act between two people who really loved each other.

I lay back on the bed when we had finished. I felt so content. She was the loveliest person in the whole world.

'You need to take the priest's advice,' Carole-Anne said.

'What?' I asked. I was stunned. How did she know?

'You need to take Fr Gallagher's advice,' she said again.
'How do you know?' I asked directly.
'I know everything,' Carol-Anne said.
'How?'
'I know everything,' she said again. But her voice was fading.
'How?' I demanded. 'You could be in danger,' I advised.
'I know everything,' she whispered.
'What do you know?' I asked.
'Everything.'
I heard a noise in the room behind me, and I jumped.
'Are you alright there, John?' someone asked. It was Kieran's voice. I was just about to ask how he got into the room while I was in such a compromising position with Carole-Anne, when I opened my eyes.
I had been dreaming.
'Are you alright?' Kieran asked, as he stood over my seat in the lounge.
'Jesus,' I said, 'I was dreaming.'
Kieran laughed: 'you were groaning and mumbling. For a moment there, I thought you had helped yourself behind the bar.'
'I'd be so lucky,' I said. 'I just had a beautiful, but bizarre, dream.'
'That's what island life does to outsiders,' Kieran explained. 'Sometimes the dreams can be very penetrating and they might even scare you.'
'This one did for a moment,' I explained. 'I was being told to listen to some advice by someone who didn't even know that I had a problem.'
'Don't be telling Brigid,' Kieran said. 'She'll be telling you that it's the fairies trying to sort out your problems for you.'
Kieran paused for a moment. He had been with Brigid while I was asleep.

'So you have a problem,' Kieran said. 'Brigid said you had a chat with the priest.'

'Yeah,' I said, 'but nothing I can't handle.'

'They call him "the wise one" around here,' he said. 'You're as well to listen to him.'

'I am trying to take his advice on board,' I explained. 'As soon as I get on board the ferry first, I'll be in a better position to listen to the "the wise one".'

'Good,' Kieran said. He lowered his tone a little, and then added: 'About my cheer this morning, I want to apologise to you if that caused you offence.'

'It was nothing really,' I said. 'You're young. When you know more about work and life, you'll see the error of your ways.' I smiled as I spoke, since I knew that my patronising remark would annoy Kieran.

But he said nothing. He went to the bar, and began to stack some pint glasses into the dishwasher. He seemed to be readying the bar for another onslaught that evening from the locals.

I looked out at the ravaging sea, which was tossing and turning as if it was having a bad dream too. Though mine wasn't too bad of a dream. It was quite charming really. I loved the sex with Carole-Anne. It excited me just to think of it. She was a good-looking woman, and a very caring and sensitive one to boot. She was my type of woman, even if I would probably never see very much of her again.

Brigid arrived soon after Kieran wakened me. She was carrying some shopping, and she advised me that the word in the village was that the ferry wouldn't come back to the island that evening. I was to wait for another day at least before I got back to the mainland.

I had a beautiful meal that evening, prepared by the chef, who lived locally. In actual fact, he was a fisherman in his heyday, but had injured his leg, and was unable to go on the boats. I was introduced to him and we spoke briefly. He was a jolly man with a bad temper at times, but he cooked a very good meal for me and for a few of the locals who ate there that Monday night.

I retired to my room shortly after dinner. I tried to sleep but I wasn't tired due to my little nap in the lounge in the afternoon. Taking a copy of the Gideon New Testament from my bedside drawer, I went back to the lounge, and sat at the window, watching the sea toss and turn.

Brigid and Kieran were busy at the bar, and I could hear them chatting about this and that as the evening progressed.

I had to get my mind around my problem again, I thought. I had first of all to see my problem through the eyes of Christ and not as an accountant. The problem was that I was an accountant, even though my stay in the village was wearing those memories thin.

'What would Jesus do?' I asked myself again. He would have recognised that there was a core corruption involved in me being in the office and working on the very job that entailed selling my soul to the IRA.

Jesus would never allow himself to sell his soul. Though he would have experienced such a situation, especially when he was tempted by the devil before his ministry began, and when he was confronted by Pontius Pilate before his crucifixion. I read my Gideon New Testament for a moment.

When the devil had asked Jesus to worship him, and he would receive all the kingdoms of the earth, Jesus told him more or less to get lost, since he had his God to worship.

There was a certain parallel when Jesus was asked by Pontius Pilate if he was the Son of God, and he replied that he was. Jesus had denied the Roman gods and put faith in his own God. He had denied the satanic Roman gods who would deliver the world and worldly things to their people.

Jesus rejected Satan and re-affirmed his own belief in his God, his father in heaven.

It struck me then that I had a choice to make. The choice was between doing what Jesus had done or accepting that Satan ruled the world and that I might as well worship the devil.

It was a hard choice to make, funnily enough. Sometimes it was hard to know who ruled the world when people like big Tom Brennan could get away with no jail after attempting to launder money for the IRA. There was so much violence in the North that sometimes all the good people stayed silent for so much of the time that one could question whether they had any influence or not on the proceedings.

It was often said at mass that good always wins in the end. Did it really always win? There were people who put their two fingers up to "good", while at the same time assuring us that they were fine upstanding members of the community, and they seemed to get away with this most of the time.

Yet these people were pathetic too, when I thought about it. They would like us to believe otherwise. They would like us to believe that they had a cause and that they were the noble warriors fighting for that just cause. To me they weren't. To me, the end did not justify the means, rather the means destroyed the end when the means was violence.

My choice was to be like Jesus. I rejected the worldly goods that the IRA offered me in the form of a pay increase, as my friend Danny had offered me back in Derry. I rejected that as it made me a prostitute, and it damned me to a hell where I couldn't live with myself.

If I were to accept their offer, and was consequently "bought off", then I would not have been able to confront myself if I saw a child, or even a parent, murdered in some attack of the IRA on the British presence in Ireland.

I was not part of their machine and I would never be beholden to anything that they offered my community. I was so angry after acts of violence at times that I would sometimes promise myself that if they achieved a united Ireland, as they desired, then I would leave Ireland and make my home elsewhere.

The IRA was an evil organisation, built upon the "noble" ideal that evil was more powerful than good. It was built upon the fallacy that everyone was evil except Irish republicans, and that they were fighting for justice and goodness.

What they were fighting for was a noble ideal, the reunification of Ireland, but it was only noble in that it brought together the divided peoples of Ireland. The violence simply could not achieve that, and on the contrary it led to a wedge being driven between those same divided peoples.

The IRA was evil. It wouldn't be the first evil organisation in the history of mankind to believe that it was truly good. And it wouldn't be the last in all probability.

But evil it was. It even had the sheer in-your-face arrogance to elect a Sinn Fein leader who was once the commander of the most notorious brigade in the IRA - Gerry Adams. This man was truly deluded if he felt that he could unite the divided peoples of Ireland.

Yet he wasn't there to unite them. He was there to defeat the unionists. He was there to provoke them into making themselves out as bigots, and thereby undermine support for their position in the wider world.

The sheer bravado of this approach meant that most Sinn Fein voters couldn't see through the charade, and felt that if Gerry Adams can look good in the face of the unionists, then he must be the right man to do the job.

It was sheer cynicism. There was deep cynicism in Sinn Fein, I knew that. But the Sinn Fein voters were also cynical. They had been converted to cynicism by Gerry Adams' party.

They were not going to convert me to cynicism. I was going to triumph over the temptation to give in to their authority. I was going to tell the devil to get lost. That's what Jesus had done, and he was right. If it meant beginning my career over again then I would do that. No-one was going to make me part of the evil and absurd conspiracy to use violence to unite people.

I was my own man, and I would remain my own man, not some stooge existing on the edge of a movement where gangsters and murderers held the sway.

They could ask me if I was the Son of God, just as Pontius Pilate had asked Jesus, but I would never deny that mankind was the child of the one true God. Human beings were the children of God and if that meant that I was the son of God, then so be it.

That one true God was not the creation of republicans, nor were they acting in accordance with His will. The republicans worshiped a different kind of God, one that allowed them to assume that they were righteous people who had been treated so unjustly that they had the right to destroy human life in furtherance of their position.

They had no such right in my opinion. They effectively rejected God in favour of a man-made theology that defined God in human terms, rather than in the terms that He Himself asked us to define him.

God asked us to define Him as immortal, in giving Jesus his resurrection, and we had to accept that he would not see the world through the eyes of people who were afraid of death. It was very clear to me now. Those who used violence had an inordinate fear of death and its consequences.

God had not got that fear. He was immortal and all-powerful, and yet he allowed man free will. He was a caring and responsible God, who expected us to be caring and responsible people. When we killed other human beings or supported it, we said that we wanted to end humanity.

To kill someone else, or to attempt to legitimise it, was ultimately an act of suicide. They wanted God to end the world.

They wanted God to commit suicide. They defined God as someone who was afraid of death, and they tempted him to end it all "if he has the guts".

They were, in effect, putting it up to God that they were prepared to end the world and so should he. They were saying that the world is so imperfect, and the God who created it so imperfect, that the final and only solution was to end it.

Of course, republicans, with their limited abilities, didn't see it that way. They were afraid of death, so afraid that they assumed that everyone else was afraid of death too, and that their violence was effective in changing human beings.

What God would see was different. He would see republicans as influenced by the devil to tempt him to end His own creation. He would see the republicans, and all who believed that killing human beings was an effective measure, as the devil.

I was seeing things very clearly then. Those who use violence to terminate the lives of human beings were attempting to tempt God into ending mankind. They were in effect the devil. Mankind was capable of being evil, and thus mankind had an elemental understanding of evil. They had eaten the fruit of the tree of knowledge of good and evil, and they practised both good and evil.

However, when man used violence to end God's creation, human beings, certain men defined themselves as evil. It was such an important act that it created a definitive definition of certain men as evil. It led God to consider suicide, defining as it did God as having chosen evil, by creating an evil mankind.

It defined God's profound act of love for humankind in creating man as evil, and ultimately it defined God as evil. Anyone confronted with those "facts" was bound to consider suicide, which in God's case was the ending of the world.

I didn't want the world to end. My choice had to be to refute the republican temptation of God to commit suicide, and reaffirm my commitment to life. The best way to do that was to reaffirm my opposition in the strongest possible terms to the republicans and all they stood for.

I had to refute Satan and all he stood for, and thus I had to reject the satanic ways of Irish republicanism. That meant making changes to the way I conducted my life.

Chapter Sixteen

Strange as it may seem, Carole-Anne actually appeared at the hotel later that evening. She was dressed in a denim shirt and a pair of jeans. She had come to see if I had left on the ferry earlier that day. She was a bit embarrassed to find that I was actually sitting in the lounge, listening to her enquiries.

'I'm over here,' I shouted. 'Come and sit down.'

She joined me, her face red with embarrassment that I had caught her out. She tried to apologise for being indiscreet, but she didn't need to. I was flattered.

'I hope you don't think I was looking for something from you,' she said. 'I was simply wondering whether you had got your boat.'

'Oh, I know,' I smiled.

'No, I mean it,' Carole-Anne protested. 'I was only getting the latest from Kieran and Brigid.'

'Don't worry,' I said. 'Your secret's safe with me.' She laughed and I laughed. We kind of liked each other, and we both knew it. The glances and general chit-chat at her home earlier that day had made us quite familiar.

'It's a good job I didn't get over on the ferry,' I said, smiling.

'Why not?' she wondered.

'Well,' I said, 'let's just say that I found out why your tea was so beautiful.'

'Oh,' she cried, blushing again. 'I'll get that Brigid one. Giving all my secrets away.'

'Thank God she did,' I said. 'I can just imagine explaining myself to the Circuit Court judge, that all I had drunk was a cup of tea in your house. The judge would have laughed me out of court, and fined me twice as much for lying as well as drinking and driving.'

'You only had a little,' Carole-Anne protested.

'A little poteen,' I protested, smiling. 'That's rocket fuel. I hear they have a supply at Cape Canaveral.'

'You city boys,' Carole-Anne said gently, 'just can't hold your drink. It's always the same. You think you can, but you can't.'

I noticed that Carole-Anne was drinking a pure orange drink, and that she was trying to hide it from my eyes by putting her fingers over the glass.

'It's all very well you saying that us city boys can't hold our drink, when you're sitting there with a pure orange,' I told her, jabbing away at her with my smiles.

'I'm driving,' she said. 'And I don't intend to stay long.'

'Why don't you stay the night, sure,' I said, forgetting myself for a moment.

'That's another thing about you city boys,' Carole-Anne laughed. 'You think that you can get any woman into bed.'

'I didn't mean it like that,' I said. 'You could stay over and rest from your mother for a night.'

'No,' she said. 'That's not really on. But I could stay late, if you want.'

I saw a twinkle in Carole-Anne's eye as she spoke. It was the kind of twinkle that exposes a raw nerve in you and at the very least makes you think that this woman hasn't had sex for a while. At most it scares the shit out of you since you feel that you're about to be mauled by a sex-starved nymphomaniac, who looks as if she has the strength of a lion.

As it turned out, I had at least found out her real reason for appearing at the hotel that evening. She wanted a bit of nookie. She wanted to see if the man whom she thought had fancied her in her mother's bungalow would be available for her to have a bit of fun.

'But I want to sit chatting first,' she added purposefully.

I liked Carole-Anne. She had character. She didn't mind me

having a pint, but it must have brought back memories of her ex-husband, and his problems with the drink. She was a country girl, who had lived in the big city and who was quite worldly in her own way.

But she didn't drink herself that night, even though she would have "an odd tipple" at home, and occasionally in the pubs.

We chatted for another hour. I found out so much about the island, and of how it was very special to Carole-Anne. When she had grown up on it, she hated being on the island with the storms and the lack of a proper ferry service. But later, when she had left the island, she had realised that she had had a very special upbringing in one of the most beautiful areas of the world.

She had been among such good people and she had taken for granted their goodness. The people of the island looked out for each other, and all the children were regarded as everyone's child. The adults had protected the innocence of the children, and they had guided them to maturity in "a natural paradise" off the coast of Ireland.

Her time in Dublin had been adventurous at first. She worked as a nurse in a major hospital and had witnessed much of the bad side to the capital. But as time went on, she started to realise that the bad side had a habit of getting infected into her life.

First it was boyfriends who tried to use and take advantage of what they saw as her naivety, but which was really just her good nature.

I could see that Carol-Anne was nobody's fool. She knew all the tricks of the trade, so to speak, and she could handle herself as well as any woman that I had ever known. But she wasn't battle hardened. That was a pleasant surprise. She still felt the pain of the suffering of her mother, and even of the fisherman who had been winched to safety from the boat onto the helicopter in the rescue that I had witnessed, and who was reputed to have nearly lost his arm.

Eventually she got up. I thought that she was going to the toilet, but she said it was late and she had to be getting back to her mother. But she winked at me, and I knew that it was a cue to get up to leave her to the door without arousing the suspicions of the islanders sitting around us in the lounge.

As soon as we got out of sight of the people in the lounge, she put her arms around my neck and kissed me.

'Take me to your room,' she said.

I took her to my room, and as soon as I had locked the door behind me, she got onto the bed and lay on top of it. She was a fine figure of a woman, solid and strong but with curves in all the right places.

I lay down beside her. I didn't know what to expect since no woman had ever been so forward with me before.

Immediately she began to undress me, beginning with my shirt. As she undid the buckle of my belt, she massaged my body with a softness and tenderness that wasn't matched by all of me.

I was ready for action. I grabbed her in my arms and pulled up her denim shirt, undid a few buttons, so that it slid up her body, over her head, and fell to the ground. I snapped off her bra in an instant, so practised was I at that feature of love-making.

I groped her firm, if soft, breasts. She was a fine figure of a woman indeed. I kissed her on the nipples. She was aroused and mad for sex.

We made passionate love on the bed, on the floor and finally in the shower. She was either the most passionate woman in the world, or the most sex starved person in Ireland.

I could tell that she missed the sex and the passion. I felt so wound up when I was with her, as if her eagerness to have sex was contagious. But I liked her. She had spirit, and she was soft and tender in her heart.

I could see that she missed Dublin and maybe even her husband. I tried to tell her this before she left.

'I don't miss him,' she said. 'I miss another man who I met along the way, and he was very sexual with me. I loved him, but I could never love my husband now. He was a bastard.'

'You were having an affair then?' I wondered.

'You could say that,' she said. 'But I don't think I was ever married. I never really loved him.'

She left shortly afterwards, making her way to her car, and discreetly driving away into the night.

I was wrecked. She had been a very energetic lover. She was the kind of woman who would survive easily in the big city, so long as she was careful who she made love with. She felt safe with me. I could tell. But I was more or less a stranger with a secret on her island.

My secret was that I was effectively on the run from the IRA. I wasn't trying to romanticise my dilemma by suggesting to myself that I was "on the run". I *was* on the run. There was no doubt about that.

The IRA were trying to put pressure on me to say nothing about big Tom Brennan's tax case, and I had moved out of their reach. I wasn't afraid of them. They could do nothing to me without arousing the suspicions of the police that my death had been related to something I was working on in the office.

I was safe on the island. I was well catered for too, with friends and a lover. I could have stayed there for a long time.

I woke early again the following morning. My pubic hair was itchy and I felt for one terrifying moment that I had acquired a dose of "the crabs" from Carole-Anne. I was especially terrified since I was stuck on the island without a pharmacy and without any possible treatment for this infuriating condition.

Luckily, after a good scratch, I found that I was all right. There were no "crabs". It was just sweat, making me feel itchy.

I had a shower, and went to see if there was any breakfast ready. Kieran was standing at the bar, counting the takings for the previous night.

'Good morning,' he said cheerfully, grinning from ear to ear.

'What's rattled your cage?' I asked, attempting to keep my secret rendezvous with Carole-Anne a secret.

'Oh, nothing,' he said. 'I just thought that you'd be smiling this morning.'

'Why?' I wondered.

'You had a good chat with Carole-Anne last night,' he said. 'I was watching you from the bar.'

'And so...' I said. 'What of it?'

'Ah, come on, John,' he said. 'You can keep secrets from the rest of the punters in the bar, but you can't keep secrets from the staff.'

'What secrets?' I wondered, not wanting to endanger Carole-Anne's reputation.

'Well,' he said, 'Carole-Anne's car didn't leave here until well after you left the lounge together.'

'I was chatting to her in my room,' I protested with a smile on my face that gave away the fact that I was having a secret rendezvous with her.

'You can fool some of the people some of the time,' Kieran continued, 'but you can't fool all of the people all of the time.' We both laughed.

'She's a fine filly,' I said.

'Hurray,' he shouted, 'he's admitting it at last. And she's a fine filly. Did you get a good buck from her?'

'Not bad,' I said. I beckoned him closer with my eyes: 'I don't want you to mention this to anyone. You know how these countrywomen are about their reputations. She would tear my balls off.'

'Don't worry,' Kieran said. 'She's one of us. She's a family friend, and we'll take good care of her.'

I ate breakfast soon after, and Kieran filled me in on some of things that had happened in the lounge and in the village the previous night. There had almost been a fight in the lounge due to one villager getting very drunk, and taking out his frustrations on another punter.

In the village there were early rumours that the ferry would be over soon, and as I looked out the hotel window, sure enough, the ferry was making its way across to the island. It was a pleasant sight.

I got my things together, and went to reception to pay my bill for the previous night, having paid for the night before that already. As I strolled down to the pier, however, the wind was getting up.

I looked out to the sea and I could see the ferry being tossed around, as if it wasn't best suited to the weather conditions. It looked as if the ferry was going to have to turn back. I was keen to leave, and so I persevered down to the pier and watched developments from there.

The wind was getting stronger as I arrived there. But the ferry was still attempting to berth on the island. It struggled into the small harbour and the harbour walls prevented it from feeling the full force of the winds and the angry sea.

Some passengers got off. I was immediately shocked: one of them was my friend Danny, who had attempted to offer me a pay rise for services rendered in keeping silent about the IRA money.

'John,' he shouted. 'We thought you were over here. The Guards found your car in Burtonport. Your family are worried about you.'

'Fuck,' I thought. I forgot about my parents. I should have telephoned to tell them where I was and that I was just taking a few days off work. They didn't know where I was, and they must have been worried. But I wasn't letting Danny off the hook.

'I'll deal with my family,' I said. 'But I know it's not the reason why you're here. You can fucking stay here. I'm going back on the ferry.'

Danny approached me and whispered in my ear: 'We'll find you wherever you go. We have men in Burtonport, who're to deal with you, should we not arrive back.'

'You'll do fuck all to me,' I said. 'You can't do a damn thing. I have you all by the balls.'

'You know that might seem true to you,' Danny said. 'But it's not the situation. We're powerful enough to let a few men go in Belfast, even if it's only to set the record straight with a bastard like you. But let's not fight about this.'

'Yeah,' I said, attempting to get on the boat. 'Let's not fight. You'd only lose.'

As I stepped onto the ferry, the captain grabbed me by the arm, and told me that there would be no more sailings until the storm calmed down again.

'We nearly didn't make it there,' he said. 'That storm is very dangerous. It's going up and down like a yo-yo.'

I walked back intending to go to the hotel again. But this time, Danny and two other men were shadowing me. I could only pray that the ferry would make another crossing later that day.

I hurried up the slope to the hotel, and had a word with Brigid as soon as I got there.

Danny didn't appear at the hotel. He seemed to have remained in the village and was probably sitting in a pub, thinking that I would be back down for the ferry.

I was now in a thorny situation, as I had to pass Danny and his cronies in order to get to the pier for the ferry. Sooner or later, I was going to have to do it.

Chapter Seventeen

It was Tuesday evening. The IRA team assigned to my case must have been sitting in the bar in the village scanning the pier to ensure that I didn't slip by since they didn't appear at the hotel. The ferry wasn't going across until the morning.

Brigid was getting anxious, as I had relayed the whole story to her. She hated the IRA, but Kieran was excited that real live IRA men were in the village. It confirmed my suspicions about his upbringing, that he wouldn't have known an IRA man if one jumped up and bit him in the ass.

'I'll telephone Carole-Anne,' Brigid said eventually. 'She is more worldly. She'll known what to do.'

I couldn't help feeling that Brigid's real reason for telephoning Carole-Anne was to ensure that I didn't stay in the hotel that night. She probably didn't want any bloodshed, or any kind of trouble, that might give the hotel a bad reputation among the locals.

I couldn't complain. I had brought this upon myself, and them. They were bystanders, who might become participants, in a feud between a stranger they hardly knew and a group of thugs who might break his legs in front of them.

Carole-Anne arrived at the hotel shortly after Brigid's telephone call.

'What's the problem?' she asked. She looked at me and said: 'I thought you'd be gone by now.'

'The IRA is after him,' Brigid roared.

'Jesus,' she yelped and, as she turned to me, she lowered her voice and added: 'And I thought he was complaining of having a dose of the crabs or something.'

I laughed. It was a nervous laugh, but at least I could see the funny side of this island woman.

'I need to stay with you tonight,' I suggested.

'Why on earth?' she wondered.

'There's a couple of IRA men on the island,' I explained.

'Three,' Brigid interjected.

'And they're interested in harming me,' I continued.

'But my mother,' Carole-Anne said.

'Is there anywhere I can stay?' I asked abruptly. My desperation melted Carole-Anne's reluctance to put me up.

'Come with me,' she said. 'I can tell my mother that you're a friend from Dublin, but you've got to play along.'

I was delighted to leave the hotel. We drove quickly around the back of the island so that the IRA men couldn't see us pass through the village. We arrived at Carole-Anne's home and we rushed into it.

'Mammy's in bed,' she said. 'but she might get up for an hour later on.'

I checked the road behind us to ensure that we were not followed. Then I sat down on the couch while Carole-Anne made a cup of tea.

Eventually Carole-Anne sat down beside me.

'So tell me what the problem is, John,' she said. 'You know, I could tell that you had a problem last night.'

'How?' I wondered, my face becoming redder by the moment. What was my problem last night, I wondered.

'You weren't at your best,' she said. 'You were a little preoccupied. I could tell.'

'I hadn't really got a problem last night,' I protested. 'They arrived over on the ferry today. I was safe last night on the island.'

'You were safe with me,' Carole-Anne said. 'And you're safe with me tonight.'

Fuck, I said to myself, noting the twinkle in her eye again. She wants more tonight.

'And what's more,' she added. 'We've got a lot more time

tonight.' She really did want more. I was going to be pretty tired in the morning.

I tried to explain to her about the funds that I had accidentally come across that had belonged to the IRA, and that they were trying to keep me quiet in relation to them. She wasn't concerned about the reason I was staying at her home. She was simply enthralled at the prospect of a man being available to her for two nights running.

'We're going to have some fun tonight,' she kept saying as she caressed my thigh.

I admired her enthusiasm, but I was tired. I had been worrying all day about what I might do to escape the attentions of the IRA. She didn't seem to understand.

Her mother never appeared, and possibly Carole-Anne had put her off coming out to meet me. Carole-Anne took her a cup of tea and some toast late in the evening, and that was the last we heard of her that night.

Carole-Anne made herself comfortable by lying across my lap after she returned from her mother's room, and massaging the back of her head into my groin. I was facing another night with her whether I liked it or not, I feared.

Then she got up and made her way to her bedroom. She came out ten minutes later with nothing on but a little negligee. She was looking very well so far as I was concerned at that moment.

I got up and followed her into her room, where she slipped off the negligee and lay on the bed. I got on the bed beside her and we kissed and cuddled for a while before massaging each other's bodies.

I had still got my trousers on when she slipped her hand down to feel my groin. My penis was lying sideways, in an erect position, across the front of the inside of my trousers. She didn't seem able to find it.

I was trying to put her off sex and so I didn't mind. She lay back after her search for my penis and sighed.

'Don't worry, John,' she said innocently, 'it can happen to anyone.'

'What?' I wondered.

'When I was a nurse,' she said, 'I heard stories of how bad it can get.'

'What can get?' I demanded to know.

'Your man's problem,' she finally said. She was clearly implying that I had erectile dysfunction.

'Goodness,' I gasped, 'it's not that. I just don't want to have sex, that's all.' I paused and thought about her words for a moment. Clearly she had been trying to find my penis in my pants and had concluded that I was not excited. I had "a horn which would have whipped an ass from a bog", as a friend used to say to me at college.

I pushed her onto her back, and we made love again and again. She was indeed a fine filly.

We got up very early the following morning, partly because Carole-Anne wanted to look in on her mother, and partly because we wanted to be sure to get me onto any ferry that was leaving the harbour.

When we had finished breakfast, Carole-Anne took me to the village where there were a few fishermen contemplating taking out their boats. The wind had died, but fears of the storm beginning again were still on their minds.

Fortunately for me, one of the fishermen said that he was taking his boat across to the mainland in order to get parts, and Carole-Anne suggested that he take me across.

So I bade farewell to Carole-Anne with a warm embrace and kiss, promising to return one day, thanking her for her hospitality, and loving her for the "extras".

I looked up at the hotel where no doubt Danny and his friends had stayed the night, and I was glad that I was leaving the island.

'So did you have a good time?' the fisherman wondered.

'Oh, yeah,' I said. 'I had a good time alright.'

'Carole-Anne is a fine woman,' he told me.

'She is indeed,' I said. 'She's a very fine woman.'

'I'd have married her myself,' he said, 'only she ran off to that bloody Dublin.'

'Is that right?' I said. 'Do you not like Dublin?'

'I don't like cities,' he said, in his big strong Donegal accent. 'There're too many bastards around.'

I felt myself shrink as he spoke. I thought he was referring to me as a bastard.

'How do you know?' I asked. 'I'm from Derry and it's all right there.'

'I don't mean Derry,' he said, his voice heavy with anger. 'I mean real big cities. I know because I went to New York once, and I was mugged before I left the airport.' I thought that it must have taken a brave man to mug this fisherman, but he continued: 'I beat the shit out of the mugger, and got myself three months in jail. As I say, there are too many bastards in the big cities.'

He was right. If you were going to meet a bastard then it would be in the big cities. There were plenty of bastards around Belfast. There were some in Derry too, and I knew only too well that there were some who lived in the bigger towns around Northern Ireland.

Big Tom Brennan was a case in point. He was a bastard alright. He was the bastard who had gotten me into the situation I was now in, with the IRA breathing down my neck and attempting to bully me into keeping silent about their money.

'How's the fishing at this time of year?' I asked the big Donegal man out of curiosity. His boat was relatively small and could only really have been used for small catches.

'Crabs and oysters,' he explained, 'are easy to catch about now. But the bloody weather is making it difficult. It's the same every winter these years.'

'Could a man make a living out of it?' I enquired, thinking in my professional capacity that it must be a very poorly paid job.

'You city boys,' he said, with a little anger, 'all you want to know about is the money. This is my livelihood, and it was my father's and grandfather's livelihoods, and we were born to be on the sea. It's all we know. And it's the greatest knowledge of all. No-one, but God Himself, will get us off these boats.'

'I didn't mean to inquire about money,' I said. 'But the fishing is something that I've always felt an attraction to. I was wondering if it was worth my while.'

The big fisherman laughed. He took me by the hands and turned them over so that he could see the palms.

'These hands,' he roared, trying to contain his laughter, 'are the hands of an office worker, who sits at a desk all day, and, if you don't mind me saying so, who plays with himself at night.'

That was a bit near to the bone. I laughed for fear that he would throw me off his boat if I didn't. He was a thick man, but a sensible one. He knew what he wanted in life, and he had it. At least he had his pride. I was wondering where mine had gone and his insult that I played with myself at night really rankled.

I promised that I would tell him that in no uncertain terms as I got off his boat. I had my speech prepared: 'You can well say that I play with myself, but it's better than playing with a cod slice up the back of your boat.' That would annoy him, I thought.

But I never did get to say my piece to him. He was a decent enough man to give me a lift, and too thick to play games with in reality. So I disembarked from his boat, thanking him for the lift and telling him that I hoped the weather improved.

I was also concerned that I would run into more IRA men waiting for me in Burtonport. I thought that at the very least they would have let my tyres down on the car, or slashed them.

I approached my car anxiously from the pier and found it sitting there in the market square, untouched. I was relieved. I decided to get out of there as fast as I could.

I drove south out of Burtonport, since it was the only road that didn't lead to Derry. Though I wasn't quite sure where I was going. I hoped that I would come out at Donegal town on the southern tip of the county.

I drove and drove, stopping only once for petrol. Eventually I came out at Ballybofey on the road between Derry and Donegal town. I stopped there for a cup of tea.

I went into a little coffee shop in the town centre and sat watching out the window in case my IRA friends would catch up with me. I was satisfied that I was well ahead of them, even if they had boarded the first ferry from Aranmore that morning. I had at least an hour on them.

I had my cup of tea and I thought about my predicament. The anger was welling under the surface. Here I was, involving decent Aranmore islanders in my problems, and getting them mixed up in God knows what. I didn't know all the implications of the money held in offshore accounts on behalf of the Provisional IRA. Perhaps there was more to it than the reputation of big Tom Brennan, or the fact that he might go to jail. Perhaps a lot of people would go to jail.

'The fuckin' IRA,' I roared to myself as I sat in the coffee shop. 'They fuckin' ruin everything.'

'Did you say something?' the lady in the shop asked.

'No,' I said. 'It's just so cold this morning. Isn't it?'

I was determined to confront the bastards, whatever it took. They were not going to ruin my life.

I set off in my car, back in the direction of Derry. It was the safest place to be when confronted by the IRA. They couldn't do anything there without there being a major fuss kicked up by the local political and Church establishment.

I was almost gasping at my innocence on Aranmore island, where I had assumed that I was safe in Carole-Anne's home. I hadn't been safe. Kieran would have told the IRA where I was, and taken them there if they needed to go.

I was totally trapped on an island with strangers, and if I had been tracked down, they could have killed me without so much as a word from the outside world. The islanders might have been ignored as they had been for a long time, and the guards might have ignored their pleas for an investigation.

It had been a nightmare, and yet there I was, safely and warmly tucked up beside Carole-Anne in bed. I laughed. Carole-Anne was some mover! She was the kind of girl you'd been longing to meet but weren't quite happy with once you'd done so.

But she had been a life-saver for me. She had saved my life as surely as she had taken a bullet for me. I cringed when I thought of her taking a bullet. I hoped and prayed that Danny would leave her alone, now that I was gone.

I could never be sure with the IRA. They were a strange organisation. They damned mankind to death by killing one person.

It was time to face the devil back in Derry.

Chapter Eighteen

'The fuckers,' I roared on entering my apartment in Derry. It had been ransacked. The IRA must have been searching for something there.

They hadn't done much damage in reality, and their search had been pretty timid in comparison to some that I'd seen in the movies. But it was the thought that they been in my personal space. They had violated my personal environment in a way that suggested that they intended to scare me more than anything else.

'Right, this means war,' I shouted as I entered my bedroom and saw the wardrobes upended and the bed bare as if they had torn everything off it. I was going to kick ass. Well, I was going to do something. I couldn't allow these bastards to get away with their attempt at intimidation.

But I ruled out a direct confrontation.

I wasn't going to fight with their muscle in the street. I was not some cur dog. I was a professional man with professional ethics and a professional training. I was going to use that against them.

I was going to scare the shit out of them in the way that they had scared me. But I was going to do it in such a way that would worry the thinkers in their organisation.

The first thing I would do was report the burglary at my flat to the RUC. When the republicans heard that I was consorting with the enemy, they would get worried, and they would come running to me.

So I telephoned the police, leaving my apartment as it was in order to maximise the effect on the coppers. It was a while before they arrived.

'So what's been taken?' a copper asked me after surveying the scene on his arrival. I baulked at his question, as I hadn't thought of looking.

'I don't know,' I said. 'Perhaps they didn't take anything, but look at the state of the place. They were here for a reason.'

'Okay, sir,' he said. 'Take a look again and see if anything was stolen. You'll need details for insurance purposes. Meanwhile I'll have a look around.'

There was evidence of a break-in in one of the bedrooms of my ground floor apartment. The copper noticed it as soon as he entered the bedroom.

'Here's where they got in,' he said, pointing to the window, which looked as if it had been cracked. On closer inspection, it was clear that I needed a new pane of glass. A corner of the old pane was missing and the thief had simply opened the larger window after cracking open the smaller one.

'It's a pretty professional job,' the copper said. 'But thieves aren't usually so untidy.'

He scanned the rest of the apartment for clues, and told me that the fingerprint department would be up later to see if they could get prints from the window.

Eventually he turned to me and asked nonchalantly: 'Do you have any enemies, sir?'

'No,' I replied. 'I live and work in Belfast during the week, and I can't see any way that any enemies would go this far to seek retribution.'

'But you have enemies?' the copper asked rhetorically.

'Only the usual,' I replied. 'You know, people I've fallen out with over the years.' I didn't want to be too definitive with the copper as I realised that I might have to get back to him later about the IRA intimidation.

'What about paramilitary organisations, sir?' he asked abruptly. I was shocked by his question. Was it that obvious? Had they left clues?

'How do you mean?' I asked nervously. 'Is there something here indicating that?'

'We can't rule it out, sir,' he said. 'You would be the best person to tell us if there is. But you can come back to us if you think of any reason.'

That was the problem. The thief had taken nothing, and the cop was right to be suspicious of paramilitary involvement. What could I say? It looked funny.

Nonetheless, the visit of the cop had served its purpose. It meant that I had been talking to the cops and, so far as the republicans were concerned, I might have been telling them all about the involvement of big Tom Brennan in their organisation. They would not be amused.

To ensure that the republicans knew, I telephoned a friend, who I knew would tell other friends very quickly that I had been robbed and had talked to the police. It wasn't going to be long before the republicans knew I was in town, and was communing with the cops.

That night, I decided to go out on the town. I met up with some friends in the Clarendon Bar at the edge of the city centre and away from republican areas. I drank a few pints telling my friends about the couple of days I had spent on Aranmore island.

'Jesus,' Peter, an artist friend, said, 'this boy's been hooring about and we've been worried that he had taken leave of his senses.'

Peter was always diplomatic, and I knew that his disposition and his words had been carefully adapted to reflect a diplomatic posture on my activities. All my friends seemed to know that I was in some kind of trouble with the IRA. It was a dangerous situation to be in, as the more people knew about my troubles, the more likely that the IRA would have to set an example with me.

I played along with Peter's diplomacy, letting on that I had been taking a winter's break during a period of holiday that was due to me.

'Carole-Anne was the finest woman I've met in a long time,' I boasted. 'She was caring and loving, and a good lay to boot.'

'Getting your oats as well,' Peter laughed. 'Why didn't you ask and I would have gone over there with you.'

'I never thought,' I said. 'I just went for a drive and ended up on an island. I was only going for a daytrip when the weather went wild and I had to stay for a few days.'

'What was the hotel like?' he asked.

'Great,' I said. 'But I was the only guest.'

'Did you meet anyone you knew?' he wondered. His question wasn't as diplomatic as the other ones. I knew what he was getting at. There were probably rumours that Danny had gone to fetch me, ostensibly on behalf of my family.

'No,' I replied, ever cautious. 'I got back over in a fishing boat, and the ferry hadn't left at that stage.' It was a simple answer that dodged the question of whether I had seen Danny and his cronies.

Then I looked around and I saw a familiar face approaching us in the crowd. It was Danny. I almost choked on my pint.

'How're the boys?' Danny asked nonchalantly.

'Not too bad,' Peter said. 'How's yourself?'

'A bit tired,' he said. 'I had a rough night's sleep last night.'

I laughed. Danny had obviously not been able to sleep in the soft beds of the hotel the previous night. I took him aside.

'What the fuck do you think you're playing at?' I asked him.

'What do you mean?' he replied.

'I mean – following me as if I was some common criminal,' I said.

'We're just keeping an eye on you,' he explained. 'You're a man with information which could damage our cause.'

'Your cause,' I said. 'Your cause is evil. You're the children of the devil.'

'Fuck off,' he said. 'You're the one who's running around like a man possessed.'

There was no getting through to a man like Danny. He had his commitments, and they coloured all he saw and thought.

'What are you lot going to do now?' I asked.

'Take you for interrogation,' he said. 'You've been talking to the RUC. You know that's not on.'

'Fuck you,' I said. 'You're not taking me anywhere.'

'We'll do it here then,' he said.

Then he began to ask questions of a revealing nature. He revealed to me that their organisation was petrified of me, and what I might do. I felt smug in the knowledge that I had them by the balls. But it still didn't seem right. Some part of their analysis was indiscernible to me. I couldn't understand why they were so wound up.

'What's your problem?' I asked.

'We have no problem,' Danny said. 'We can sort you out.'

'No,' I said, 'something's not right. Why are you so concerned?'

Danny leant up against my shoulder and whispered in my ear.

'The fucking file,' he whispered. 'We want it.'

I smiled. First, I thought that they were kidding and that they had simply misplaced the file in my office. Then I recalled that I had taken the file out of the office and to my home on the night before my last day at work. I had wanted to ensure that I was fully aware of its contents and that nothing had slipped by me. But that night I spent with Bernie had distracted me, and I had forgotten about it.

I was scared for a moment. They had been searching for big Tom Brennan's file when they burglarised my home. Then a flash of inspiration hit me. I turned to Danny.

'The file was stolen,' I said. 'Someone stole it from my apartment.'

'You bastard,' he said. 'You know it wasn't.'

'How do you know that?' I asked. 'Are you telling me that you knew the thief?'

'You know it wasn't stolen,' he said again.

I grabbed him by the throat, and told him that if he didn't get out of the bar that instant, then I would throw him out there and then.

'Don't you ever enter my home,' I bulled.

'You've got our file,' he said, pushing my hand away from his throat.

'That's right,' I said, 'but the police know it was stolen. You lot stole it.'

'Give us the file,' he roared. He had lost the run of himself. The whole bar was watching us, and I was lapping it up.

'Fuck off,' I roared, 'you Provo bastard.'

'That'll do, boys,' Peter interjected.

'That bastard has our file,' Danny roared. I was really enjoying it. They were exposing themselves by using Danny, who must have had a few drinks too many.

'The file was stolen,' I shouted. 'These Provo bastards stole it, and now they want me to give it back.'

Two men approached Danny from behind, and whispered something in his ear, and then pushed their arms under his and lifted him back into the crowd.

I was jubilant. I had outsmarted them. They had shown their hostility to me in a public place, and if anything had happened to me subsequently, then the word would have been out in the street that it had to do with a file I owed the republicans.

They couldn't harm me now. And it was all down to a file I didn't even know I had until they told me.

The file was in my briefcase, and I had left it in the boot of my car. But for all the police knew, it could have been stolen during the break-in. Instantly, I thought of a new way of punishing the republicans. I really was going to lose the file if it meant that much to them.

I was going to lose it and all my work on it, so that I could say that I had not contributed anything to the saving of big Tom Brennan from prison.

If he wanted to fly in the face of decency and reason by lodging £1,000,000 to an offshore bank account, and telling the Inland Revenue that it was from his trading, a feat that simply was not possible, then I would not be implicated in his lies.

It was a typical case of in-your-face provocation from the republicans. It was the same in-your-face provocation that Sinn Fein used to maximise its vote. They simply provoked unionists into hating them for their obvious lies, while at the same time keeping international public opinion on board, opinion that wasn't as aware as the unionists of their lies.

The average Sinn Fein voter didn't care that Sinn Fein wasn't completely honest, so long as their party supported the IRA campaign that so obviously revolted and intimidated the unionists.

In the same way big Tom Brennan didn't really care that he was caught. He possibly thought that he could get at the tax inspector before he went to the RUC Special Branch. There lay the problem for me. I hated the RUC Special Branch too, and it was in the nature of the Northern Ireland conflict that I had no-one to protect my interests when something actually needed to be investigated by an appropriate authority.

However, thinking about it rationally, it was better that I didn't side with either the forces of the state or the paramilitary forces. I was up against a loaded dice and I knew it. But at least I knew it. None of these organisations could be trusted ultimately to act in my interests. They all had their own agendas.

But it was this provocative stance of people like big Tom Brennan that really annoyed me. They really didn't care about anyone or any ideal. It was them against the rest.

The republicans had used me. I really detested that. I had seen that same attitude in politics. No-one was as clever as the republicans. They were "a movement" and as such they were bound to win in the end, they effectively said. They could use people at will, and get away with it most of the time, because they could rely on the fact that people were afraid of them. And people were afraid of them.

But I wasn't. I had them by the proverbials. They could do nothing to me. They thought they could slip big Tom Brennan's investigation by me, and that even if I discovered the anomalies, they could rely on me saying nothing. But I was made of better stuff.

I was angry that they had used me in my own office. I wanted to grab big Tom Brennan and give it to him big time. It was typical of the in-your-face arrogance of the republican movement to think that they could use just about anybody to get their way.

But now I stood in their way. Like the Manchester tax inspector, who possibly knew nothing about the possibility of IRA involvement in the "undeclared income", I stood in their way.

I was not going to back down now. I was a supporter of the SDLP, and my boss knew that. Moreover, I had reasoned that the IRA was an evil organisation when things had made sense to me on a little island off the coast of Ireland. I was not backing down now.

I was going to show them what intelligence was. I was going to show them that I would not tolerate anyone attempting to use me as a cover for their criminal activities. The IRA may well have been heroes to many republicans, but they were no heroes of mine. They were gangsters and I had the proof of that.

The first step was to get rid of big Tom Brennan's file, and claim to my boss that it had been stolen. That would take my name off the investigation, and ensure that the work on it had to be done again by some stooge elsewhere.

That was preferable to letting the republicans think that they had my tacit support for their campaign of violence against the unionists and the British. That's what I hated most: the thought of the republicans assuming that big John was a sound man really, who was fully behind the IRA.

I was going to put them off that notion.

Chapter Nineteen

The first thing I did when I got up the following morning was to visit my parent's home. I took my briefcase with me, and when I went upstairs to the toilet, I secreted the briefcase in a bedroom underneath some clothes in a wardrobe they rarely used. It would be safe there for a while, and even if they found the briefcase, my parents would know that it was mine.

Big Tom Brennan's file was inside the briefcase. I smiled when I had finished hiding it. It was a just reward for his ignorant use of me. He had to start again with us, or with a new accountant, and get his affairs into shape.

The IRA would not like it one little bit. It exposed them to the possibility that the tax inspectors in the investigation branch may see it as an obstruction of their work, or at least a desire not to cooperate fully with their team. They may then take a more proactive role in the investigation. It even risked the possibility that an astute investigator would discover that the offshore accounts were not really the profits of Big Tom's businesses.

I wondered what the IRA would do as I drove away from my parent's home, on my way back to my apartment. They could shoot me dead, but the fact was that they didn't know where I had hidden the file, and there may well have been repercussions if anything happened to me.

The file might suddenly appear and the whole IRA organisation would be in uproar to learn that they had shot dead a man because he had come across a tax file that indicated that the IRA were about to donate two million pounds to the British Exchequer.

No, the IRA wouldn't shoot me dead. They could give me a punishment beating, but they would find it difficult to justify in the public domain, and there remained the possibility that I would embarrass them with the file.

There was little they could do, I concluded.

As soon as I got home, I lifted the telephone and spoke to the police officer who had come to my apartment.

'I've just realised that my briefcase has been stolen,' I told him. 'I thought it was in my car boot, but it isn't.'

'Okay, sir,' Sergeant Roberts said. 'We'll come around and take the details later this morning.'

It wasn't that long before Sergeant Roberts arrived. He took down the details and scratched his head when he had finished.

'This important file,' he said, 'is puzzling me. You could lose your job over something like that. I know that if it happened to me, I would face severe disciplinary procedures.'

'Well,' I said, 'I don't think I'll lose my job. It was in a safe place, and I wasn't negligent.'

'But the thief,' he said, 'might not realise its value. We have to do something about that. You know what I mean - he could be about to dump it somewhere.'

'What do you suggest?' I asked.

'A public announcement,' he said. 'We'll say that the file was stolen, and is of no monetary value, but that the owner would really like it back.' He looked at me in an embarrassed kind of way, as if he wasn't really falling for my story, and added: 'You could even get your boss to give a reward to the finder of the file. It may well work.'

I didn't know whether to say something to him in order to avoid having to talk to my boss. If I said something, I might confirm his suspicion that I was not telling the whole story. If I didn't, I would have to tell Sean, my boss, about the loss of the file, something for which I was not yet prepared. I quickly decided that I would have to tell Sean sooner or later.

'Okay,' I said. 'I'll get on to my boss straight away. In fact, I'll ring him now while you're here, and you can explain the circumstances to him.'

Sean was fuming when I told him. He was as angry as he had ever been in my experience of him.

'You did what!' he kept roaring.

The police sergeant calmed him down, and told him that he had to be "constructive". I bit my tongue at that as I could guess that Sean was attempting to control his temper to a very great extent.

A reward of £1,000 was suggested for the return of the undamaged file, whatever about the briefcase. I suspected that the policeman thought I was up to no good, even though he went through the motions of believing my story. I confronted him about it as he went to make a statement to the press.

'You don't buy this, do you?' I wondered.

'I can't possibly comment,' he said.

'Come on, why not?' I wondered.

'If you were a doctor,' he said, 'a thief would want your briefcase without knowing what was in it. Drugs would be his target. But an accountant's briefcase would be worthless unless the thief knew what he was looking for.' His analysis seemed sensible. Of course, he added: 'But you never know. The thief could have thought you were a doctor.'

I smiled. I didn't want to add anything to the comments that I had already made, comments that could have implicated me in a case of wasting police time.

I listened to the radio that afternoon. The local BBC station, Radio Foyle, broadcast a statement from police in relation to my briefcase and its contents. "The contents were of no value to anyone else, but contained work carried out by an accountant. If anyone was to come across these papers, they should contact Strand Road RUC Station and receive a reward of one thousand pounds."

I laughed when I heard the statement. It seemed so bizarre. It seemed that the police were accepting my story verbatim. They had not questioned it. But why should they? I was a respected member of the community, and I had to be taken seriously.

I had no qualms about lying to the police. It got me out of a tricky situation. They were not really an acceptable police force in any case with their ongoing war with republicans and their seemingly endless ability to tar all Catholics with the same brush, and treat them accordingly.

But they were a shrewd bunch, the coppers. They would smell a rat if there was one to be smelt. I had to be careful that they didn't get close enough to smell any rats that I might have hiding under my bed. The only rat I had was the briefcase, and so far as I was concerned, at that moment, they would never see it again.

That was unless the republicans played a stupid hand, and went after me for the file to be returned.

Sean rang late in the afternoon. He was still balling and moaning about the file. He wanted me to check everywhere I had been over the weekend, since leaving the office, to see if I had left it accidentally and forgotten about it. It was no more than I expected. It was diplomatic language from Sean for, "We know you didn't lose it, so get it back here now".

Sean amused me with his words, but I could sense a profound anger in his speech that hadn't been there earlier in the day, when desperation had dominated his words.

He was going to get that file so far as he was concerned. No-one was going to find it lying in the street, or on a tip, and give it to the police. That was his greatest fear: that the police would retrieve the file and give it a once over before returning it to me. Perhaps he thought that I was threatening that by involving the police in the search for the file.

That was a frightening thought. Perhaps the IRA now thought that I was about to lay one of their senior members bare by giving the file to the RUC. That would have made me an informer, and subject to a death sentence in the Nationalist community.

I had no intention of doing that. I was simply sending out the signal that I would not be used by the IRA to do their bidding. But now I had to accept that the signal was confusing, and if they interpreted the fact that I spoken to the police as a threat of imminent action against them, and big Tom Brennan in particular, then they could take very serious action.

I was not prepared for that. For an instant, I thought, 'give the file back'. But no, they had used me. These evil bastards had used me as a cover for an investigation into a man who was helping to fund a campaign of violence in my name and in the names of other people, and they were killing people in our name. It wasn't on. They had to be stopped.

I went to a bar that night to see if I could see Danny, my solicitor acquaintance who had followed me to Aranmore. We were no longer friends. He was simply an ambassador for the republican movement, and I wanted to set a few things straight with him and his organisation.

I wasn't standing very long at the bar when there was a thud at the door, and in marched Danny with two cronies.

'What the fuck do you think you're playing at?' he asked me immediately, his buddies covering either side of me.

'Boys,' the barmaid shouted. 'There'll be no fighting in here.'

'Yeah, boys,' I said, smiling at Danny, 'you know the rules.'

'Fucking rules,' Danny gasped. 'You broke every rule in the book today.'

'I did?' I asked rhetorically.

'You fucking know you did,' Danny roared under his breath. 'Those cops are asking questions, and whatever they find, we'll take it out on you.'

'They won't find anything,' I said. 'There's nothing to find. The file is missing permanently.'

'Don't give us that shit,' Danny hissed. 'You know you're playing hardball with the IRA.'

'How?' I asked.

'You know,' Danny grunted. 'You want something in return for the file, and you won't get a penny. What you'll get is …' He stopped at that. I thought that he had finished but he nodded at the men beside me, who were sturdy men, and one of them hit me a dig in the ribs.

'You know what you'll get,' Danny roared.

'Out now,' the barmaid shouted. 'You three, get out. We don't want your sort in this bar.' She turned to me, as I held my ribs, which were quite sore, and she asked me if I was all right.

'I'll survive,' I replied, as Danny and his cronies made their way to the door.

'You have twenty-four hours,' Danny roared. 'We'll be watching you.'

The barmaid came round to me, and stood beside me at the bar.

'Who's that?' she asked.

'It was Danny Murray, the solicitor,' a bartender said from the other side of the counter. 'Isn't that right, John?'

This bartender knew our company, and he seemed to know all our names.

'Did you fall out?' the barmaid asked.

'Sort of,' I said. 'He wants something from me.'

'I'd give him whatever he wants,' the bartender said. 'He's got connections.'

'I'll think about it,' I said as I drank the last sip of my pint.

'Think about it good,' the bartender said. 'I know a fellow who squared up to Danny a few years back, and had his ankles crushed for his troubles. He never walked properly after it. Danny is a rough man.'

As I walked the short distance back to my apartment, I trembled at the thought of the bartender's words. I didn't want my ankles crushed. I wanted to walk properly for the rest of my

170

life. I especially didn't want Danny to be part of any crushing squad that might come my way.

But they meant business all right. Nonetheless, I couldn't work out how they thought that they would get away with it. I held all the cards. If they attacked me, they would leave themselves in a very precarious position. They would almost certainly put big Tom Brennan in jail.

Surely they didn't want that.

Nevertheless, it was in the nature of the republicans never to know when they were beaten. When they got into a tight situation, which they were in now, they threatened and bullied to get their way. That was their way. They knew no other way.

So I had twenty-four hours to find a means of placating them. If I didn't, they would find a way of flattening me. I didn't find the prospect of being flattened by their methodology in any way enticing. They were thugs and they had proven it beyond all reasonable doubt.

As I arrived back at my apartment, I sat and had a cup of coffee. There was a late night film on television. It was a particularly violent gangster movie. There was lots of blood and gore, and my stomach churned at the thought of my own situation, dealing with similar mean men, who would blow my head off without the slightest whim.

But that's what the Provos were, a bunch of gangsters, who were as nice as pie in front of other people in normal circumstances, but who were vicious thugs in reality when the going got tough.

I had found out more about Danny, my old friend, who drifted in and out of our company. He was a real nice guy at first sight. You would consider him harmless, and yet when all was said and done, he was a thug, ruling his fiefdom with an iron fist.

The barman knew that, and he had shared it with me only when he knew that Danny was my enemy.

The ordinary people of the city knew of the backgrounds of these IRA godfathers, and their grudges, and in normal circumstances they were afraid to speak out to people who might do something about it. It was only in circumstances where they sensed real hostility that they revealed their knowledge of the gangsters who attempted to rule over the working class areas with an iron fist.

I had now got two grudges with Danny. I had been assaulted myself, and I had heard of a man who had had the temerity to stand up to the IRA man, only to have his ankles crushed. I was going to score even on both counts.

Late that night, I decided that I'd better set Danny straight about a few things. It was after two o'clock, and the film had just finished, and I decided it was time to talk to Danny. Hopefully he would be tucked up in bed.

'Hello,' Danny said, with his best posh accent, as he answered the phone, possibly thinking that I was a client who had been taken to a police station.

'How are you, Danny?' I asked.

'You fucker,' he roared. 'You wakened me out of my sleep.'

'Good,' I said. 'Now, if you ever call the heavies in on me again, then I'll come down there and do damage to you personally.'

'Fuck off,' he said. 'You just get that fucking file.'

'Don't test me, Danny,' I said. 'You'll get an awful shock.'

He put down the phone. Now the scene was set for a showdown.

Chapter Twenty

I decided to go to Belfast the following morning. I was fed up with the harassment and the pressure that the republicans were exerting on me. I needed space to think.

I went to my lodgings in south Belfast. There was a note there from Bernie, my last girlfriend. She wanted us to meet again as soon as I came back.

I wasn't sure that I would come back, and I wasn't really sure that I could trust Bernie now. There was something about her, perhaps her sexual prowess, which made me feel that she was the type of person who associated with the wrong people and she knew more than she was telling.

My life had been turned upside down with the invasion of the IRA into my private life. They had attempted to compromise me by making me work on the case of their member, big Tom Brennan, and consequently they felt that they somehow owned me.

But I had their file now. They really didn't like that. They didn't "like it up them", as Corporal Jones used to say in "Dad's Army". But that was exactly the situation. I had it "up them".

What they really didn't like was the fact that an ordinary Nationalist would be so hostile to them that he would go so far as to risk his life in frustrating their plans. But I wasn't risking my life. Or maybe I was. I needed to think about that.

It was sensible for them not to push me too hard about the file, since I might produce it and embarrass their entire organisation. The most embarrassing thing for them was the suggestion that the IRA was dominated and controlled by businessmen and not by revolutionaries.

In that scenario, they might lose their idealistic supporters and many of their members who felt that their organisation was a pure vehicle for revolutionary change. It would be seen to be no more than a gangsters' mob, who ruled their areas without the consent of the ordinary people there.

More than that, if I defied them and gave the file over to the RUC, it would set them up to be ravaged in county Derry, where big Tom Brennan was based, and the house of cards could collapse.

So they had a right to be extremely angry about my having the file. I could create major difficulties, not least of all involving the trial and prosecution of big Tom. But why push me so hard about it?

Perhaps they thought that I would back down under pressure. They certainly indicated that the night before when one of them had thumped me in the ribs in front of witnesses in the bar.

The problem for me about backing down was that I would have no leverage over them. The file was my protection against them attempting to get at me after the affair was settled.

I could copy the file, but that meant trekking back to Derry to get it and taking it to a photocopying shop or library and risking the Provos catching me in the process. It was too risky. But they would get me wherever I went. I knew that. I had to find some way out of the situation.

They might even have arrived in Belfast and got me there. That was always a possibility. They were probably aware that I was in Belfast at that moment.

I looked out the window. There was no sign of them. I didn't think that I was followed, but they were adept at tracking me. I knew that from the island.

So what was I to do? I could sit it out and hope that they would fail to find me before their twenty-four hour deadline was up.

What could they do when their time limit was broken? They could give me a severe beating and blame it on thugs. They could get thugs to do it, and have plausible deniability on their side.

Then what could they do, having antagonised me? I could race to the police with the file and wreck all their efforts to trace it.

Of course, they might torture me until they found out where the file was and got it back. I could even face a trip to south Armagh, where the IRA did their kidnapping and torturing business. That wasn't a nice prospect. That really worried me.

I had to contact Danny again, and tell him to lift the threat. I telephoned him at his office in Derry.

'Got the file?' he asked straight off.

'No,' I said, 'you're not getting it. You have to lift the threat.'

'Then you'll give us the file?' he wondered.

'You're not getting it,' I said firmly. 'Nobody uses me. Just lift the threat or you'll find yourselves in deeper shit.'

'I'm afraid that's not possible,' he said. 'We are the ones who hold all the cards in this community.'

His reference to the community revolted me.

'You wouldn't know what community was if it jumped up and bit you,' I said.

'Don't telephone me again unless you have something to say,' he told me.

I roared at him: 'Talk to your superiors. They'll know what's good for them.' I was now in a "Cuban missiles crisis" proportions standoff with the IRA.

I waited and waited until their deadline had been reached. All the time I was thinking of a way that might placate them, and avoid a collision course. But no satisfactory means was available to me.

It was their call. They had created the crisis by setting the deadline. It was up to them to call off their hounds.

But I feared the hounds. They would not be gentle with me if they got the opportunity. They would tear into me, perhaps even moving me to south Armagh for interrogation until I revealed the whereabouts of the file.

I blocked the entrance to my room in my digs as best I could that night. I put a wardrobe and a desk against the door so that the delay in opening it would give me enough time to waken from my sleep and protect myself from their incursion, were it to happen.

I lay down with my clothes still on, ready for action. I tried to fall asleep, and though I managed a few minutes of dozing at a time, I never managed any real sleep.

I lay awake most of the time, noticing every creak outside my door, and the sound of cars and other vehicles passing by on the road outside my window. It was a tense night. I was fairly tired at the end of it, though I seemed to be full of nervous energy.

I got into my car and travelled into Belfast city centre. There was nothing happening around Belfast that day, except the usual hustle and bustle of the shoppers. I rang Bernie to arrange to meet her for lunch.

We met at a small café not far from where she worked as a waitress. I wanted to tell her how I was feeling, but though I stumbled out some words, I couldn't put them in the right order.

'You seem very tired,' Bernie smiled. 'Were you out late last night, drinking your head off?'

'I've been thinking,' I said eventually, after pausing and wondering about Bernie. She had been so good to me, and yet I had this instinctual feeling that I should not trust her.

'What about?' she laughed. 'You're not telling me that you were up half the night thinking?'

'Yes,' I explained. 'I have been.' I paused again for the words. Finally I asked her straight out: 'Can I trust you Bernie?'

'Of course,' she said flippantly.

'I mean, can I really trust you?' I sighed, interrogating her heart.

'Yeah,' Bernie said, but her tone was much less sure. I felt that she had responded to the tone of my question, and to its spirit, and become much less sure that she had my full confidence.

'I mean, can I trust you with all my heart and soul?' I asked her, gaining a psychological advantage.

'If you mean, have I been seeing someone else while you were away, then I can swear that I wasn't,' she answered.

'No, it's not that.'

'What is it then?'

'Have you been keeping an eye on me for anybody?' I asked.

'Who?' she wondered. 'Who would want to keep an eye on you?'

'The IRA,' I said. 'You know how I had the trouble in the office.'

'Yeah.'

'Well, it's got worse,' I explained nervously.

'How bad is it?' Bernie asked, almost in tears.

'It's bad,' I said. 'They could kill me.'

'John,' Bernie sobbed, 'they won't kill you.'

'How can you be so sure?' I asked.

'Look,' Bernie said as she gripped my hand tightly, 'I have a confession.' She tried to compose herself before she spoke, but as her words came out she became more emotional.

'What?' I asked.

'I am in the IRA,' she explained, her tears dripping down her face. 'I don't want you hurt. I was assigned to you. Our meeting was no accident. There are concerns that you won't play ball with us, but no-one mentioned you being killed to me.

'I like you, John, and I'm telling you this because I don't want you to get hurt. You need to be very careful with the IRA. They're dangerous people. But they operate within rules and as long as you don't break those rules, you should be okay.'

'You're IRA?' I gasped. 'For fuck sake, Bernie. Don't you realise that these people have used you more than they used me?'

'I'm a willing volunteer,' Bernie replied, wiping the tears from her eyes with a handkerchief. 'I obey my orders.'

'Orders,' I laughed angrily. 'What orders? To sleep with men like some cheap tart?'

'It's for the cause,' Bernie said. 'Look, John, if you knew what it's like in west Belfast, you would join up too.'

'I'm from Derry, Bernie,' I said. 'We have the same trouble there. We don't all join up for the cause. There are nobler causes.'

I had suspected that Bernie wasn't being straight with me when I recalled that she had offered to put me in contact with her brother, who she said had republican connections. It was a strange offer at a time when I was seeing the republicans come out of the woodwork. It was frighteningly coincidental that I had just been going out with a west Belfast girl at that time.

Bernie sat for a moment contemplating the situation. She possibly thought that I might make a scene and blow her cover as an IRA operative. But she knew me well enough to know that I didn't like scenes. She calmed herself, and used a napkin to wipe the sweat from her brow.

'There's no greater cause than ours,' she proclaimed. 'Ours is the greatest cause of all. The cause of Ireland is the cause of labour, as James Connolly said. We will achieve a thirty-two county, socialist republic.'

I laughed. It was an amusing thought. Big Tom Brennan would have a few words to say about a socialist republic.

'What are you laughing at?' Bernie asked innocently.

I looked at her in disbelief. 'If I don't laugh, I will cry. Do you know how ridiculous it is to talk in those terms in this day and age.'

'What?'

'Socialism is dead. The Soviet Union is dead. The Eastern Bloc is finished. The time for socialist republics has gone. You people are living in the past.'

Bernie didn't know what to say. It was all above her head. Eventually she managed a reply: 'Nothing will stop us getting a united Ireland.'

'Look,' I said. 'I like you too Bernie, and there's no hard feelings about our relationship. It was good while it lasted.'

'But there are things that you should know. First of all, there's very little support for a socialist republic outside the ghettos of Belfast and Derry. This war is not about socialism. It's against true socialism, if anything. Like all wars it's about businessmen and access to markets and resources. You're only kidding yourself if you think that the leaders of your organisation are not using you. They're making you into a whore.'

'Don't you dare!' Bernie shouted, making to slap me.

'Calm down,' I said, grabbing her outstretched arm. 'I'm not being personal. This war is reducing mankind in the technological age, with television and radio, to no more than a group of wild animals. It's absolutely sickening.'

'I agree,' Bernie said. 'But something has to be done.'

'Better do nothing, if "something" means killing human beings,' I said.

'Like the SDLP,' Bernie smiled. 'They do nothing, and the people suffer.'

There was no convincing Bernie of the advantage of a negotiated solution to the North's problems. I was very tired and I just gave up.

'We'll have to agree to differ,' I said. Bernie got up and we hugged and we agreed to leave it at that. She insisted however that I agree to say that her cover had not been blown, and I suggested that I would say nothing.

After lunch, I decided to travel back to Derry. It was a seventy mile trip and it took about an hour and a half. I was exhausted by the time I got to the Maiden City.

During the journey, I had tortured myself with the argument

that now was a good time to concede to the republicans. I was too tired to come to any firm conclusions, but I was prepared to ditch all my principles if the need arose. I was not going to be a martyr for some stupid file.

Yet my work was on the file, and the file contained such revealing information that anyone would conclude that only a dedicated republican should have worked on it. It was effectively an IRA file, covering the real purpose of money sent from the USA to support the cause of the IRA with a weak case for a county Derry businessman, who simply didn't have the resources to create such wealth on his own.

I arrived at my apartment, and lay down on my bed. I was so exhausted that I fell asleep immediately.

I woke at around six o'clock, feeling hungry but rested. The IRA hadn't moved on me as yet. But I knew that they would try something.

Then there was a telephone call. A prominent Derry businessman wanted to talk to me. He said he had been telephoning all afternoon, but there had been no answer.

'I want to help you recover your file,' he said, after his introduction.

'How do you know I lost a file?' I asked, quick to realise that my name hadn't been given out in the news bulletins.

'Someone told me,' he said, unwilling to elaborate.

'Who?' I asked, wanting him to reveal that he had IRA connections.

'Look,' he said, 'that's not important. I'm not against you. I want to help resolve a dispute that might bring discredit on the Catholic community, particularly the Catholic business community.'

I thought he might have an answer to my dilemma of how to get the IRA off my back and save face. 'Go ahead,' I said. 'What's your solution?'

'I'm offering ten thousand pounds to whoever retrieves the file,' he said. 'But I must make it clear that we cannot involve the RUC, as they are a hostile police force, and the thief must return it to you.'

'Ten thousand pounds,' I said. 'That's a lot of money.'

'But you have to go public that it is your file,' he explained. 'The thief must come to you and not to the RUC.'

I thought for a moment. It was a good offer if they really wanted to retrieve a file, but he had mentioned a dispute. I needed to clarify that aspect of it.

'What dispute will this resolve?' I asked coyly.

He stammered for a moment, then said: 'The dispute between you and the thief.'

I knew exactly what he was saying. He was offering me ten thousand pounds to hand the file back to my boss. He knew that I had it. That much was clear from the tone of his pronunciation of the word "thief". It was as if he meant me. He certainly didn't believe that there was a thief.

'I'll need to think about my name being used,' I told him. I took his details and said that I would contact him soon.

The businessman knew that there had been a dispute between the IRA and me. He was being coy about his knowledge of it since he probably thought his telephone might have been bugged, a usual paranoia in Derry business circles.

But he knew that I was probably looking for a way out of the dispute that he mentioned. It was a tempting offer. I was tempted, I'll admit that. But it was like Jesus in the wilderness when he was tempted by the devil.

Nothing was going to convince me of the need to give the file back. Ten thousand pounds was a lot of money then, and it still is, but I was determined to see my way through the temptations of these evil men.

They wanted me to sell my soul for ten thousand lousy

pounds. I was determined not to. It was a spit in the ocean compared to the resources that these people had. They had proved that with their loss of two million pounds to the Inland Revenue. They could easily have offered me one hundred thousand pounds. At least that amount would reflect the extent of the trouble that the file could prove to be for big Tom Brennan.

But Tom Brennan could get the work on the file done again, even in another accountancy practice. He was not completely stuck in that respect. What possibly annoyed them most was the fact that I was perceived as holding the file above their heads like a sword of Damocles. I had them by the balls in that respect.

The only leverage I had on them was that I was in possession of the file. If I accepted the ten thousand pounds, not only would I be selling my soul, I might also be selling my life down the river. They could capture me once I handed over the file, and then I might end up with concrete attachments to my feet at the bottom of Lough Foyle.

Then again, the businessman might have been a Knight of Columbanus, who pride themselves in being upstanding Christian men. He might have been prepared to guarantor that the agreement be honoured by both sides.

But he was aware of the dispute, and that made him IRA, or an IRA supporter, in my book.

I rang him back and explained that I didn't want my name to go out publicly since it would undermine my professional reputation. Diplomatically I thanked him for his efforts at attempting to resolve the "dispute", and for offering the money.

'Why not accept it, John?' he asked patronisingly.

'I would never work in this town if it were disclosed that I had lost a file worth ten thousand pounds to the business community,' I replied coyly.

'You know that's not what I mean, John,' he said, again in a patronising tone. I felt immediately that I was talking to the devil. It was just one of those feelings you get when you talk hardball with a patronising git.

'What do you mean?' I wondered, testing his patience.

'Look, I can see that I'm not going to get anywhere with you,' he said, with a little more respect and not a little anger.

'I don't think you are either,' I said, almost angrily. 'Why do you think that you can bribe someone with ten thousand pounds?'

'You know that's not what I'm talking about, John?' he said, now reciprocating my ignorance of the deal.

'Look,' I said, determined not to let him off the hook, 'some people can't be bought with money.'

'Oh, no,' he said, continuing to stick his head deliberately in the sand. 'I'm not talking about buying someone. I'm talking about persuading some petty thief to return a file that doesn't belong to him, and which he may throw on a skip and cause a friend of mine serious trouble.'

He was a consummate liar. Butter wouldn't have melted in his mouth as he spoke. The same man, I felt, would have no qualms about having someone, who he might also pay ten thousand pounds, put a bullet in the head of the "petty thief".

'Don't be wasting your money,' I said just to annoy him. 'The work could be done again in no time. Any thief who knew where the file was would have come to the police with it to receive their thousand pounds reward.'

'Yes, but we don't want that to happen, do we?' he suggested, as if assuming that I was on his side.

'I do,' I said nonchalantly. 'I'm sure you do too when you think about it.'

'No,' he said. 'I'd definitely prefer it if they came to you, rather than the discredited RUC.'

I didn't want to get into an argument about policing in Northern Ireland, and about the impartiality of the RUC in matters of non-terrorist related crime. It might have meant telling him that I felt that it was only fair that the RUC should find out about the IRA money, and that big Tom should face the same consequences as the many innocent young men from my own city who were sucked into the IRA, and faced long jail sentences because no-one was looking out for them. Indeed I assumed that people like this businessman and big Tom Brennan had sent many young men to their deaths, and to execute other innocent people, on the basis that they were worthless cannon fodder.

'We'll just have to agree to differ then,' I told him.

'I think you'll regret that course, John,' he said. It was a clear threat, but put in such a way as to cover the businessman from any possibility that the conversation was being taped.

I was now in a more precarious position, having effectively turned down the opportunity to be bought for ten thousand pounds.

I awaited their next move with baited breath.

Chapter Twenty-one

The next few days passed quickly and without incident. I was still on holiday, so I could pass the time doing whatever I wanted. The republicans seemed to be up to something, judging by the stiff stares from republican sympathisers I knew in the pubs, where I spent my lunchtimes and some evenings.

I was worried in the sense that I knew that these republicans were hostile, and that there were things being said about me. They could very well have put the word out that I had upset "the Movement", as they might say. But I knew that there was little that they could say in reality, without disclosing that their movement was losing two million pounds to the taxman. They wouldn't want their members to know about that detail. It would be really embarrassing.

One thing that really worried me was the possibility that they were badmouthing me among their membership, saying things that were untrue, in order to justify some future action. In other words, they were preparing the ground for a possible assassination attempt or some other serious action.

The only thing about that was that their cold-blooded assassins would ensure that I got the bullet on their first attempt. Thus I would get no warning, and I would be dead before the bastards walked out of my apartment, or wherever else they chose to carry it out.

By preparing their supporters for such an outcome, they would reduce the likelihood of losing support if and when public opinion and the media lambasted them. I knew this and it worried me.

My instincts said that any rational organisation would leave me alone with the file, and allow me to make my protest against being used, and carry on creating another file in another accountant's office, away from the glare of the chattering classes.

But this was the IRA. It was not a rational organisation. It dealt in vendettas, where it took it upon itself to rectify any breach of its "right" to rule its areas with an iron fist. The reality for them was that I had crossed them, and even made them look stupid and powerless, and I had humiliated them over their friend, big Tom Brennan, and they were not going to take that lying down.

Their instinct would tell them to teach me the lesson that I should never mess with the IRA. Their instinct would be to carry out some act of violence against me in order that I got the message that they ruled the Nationalist community.

They could shoot me in the ankles and elbows, in a so-called crucifixion punishment attack, but that, like all beatings, carried the risk that I would tell the RUC of the reason for the attack.

While I was thinking, it struck me that their only option was to kill me if they wanted revenge for me having humiliated them. The thought sent a chill down my spine.

On Tuesday of the second and last week of my holidays, something very strange happened. I was sitting in my apartment, reading the papers when a couple of men called to the door. I opened the door slowly and cautiously.

'Yes,' I said.

'Good morning, sir,' one of the men said. I knew immediately that they were policemen, with their proper, legalistic tone. 'We're from RUC Special Branch, and we need to talk to you.' He showed me some identification, as did the other man in turn.

'What do you want?' I asked, concerned.

'May we come inside?' the more senior officer, or at least he seemed to be more senior, asked.

'Come in,' I said, bidding them to pass me while I closed the door, and I then followed them into the living-room.

'What's the problem?' I said, thinking that the IRA might have set me up for some trouble with the RUC. I thought someone might have accused me of something.

'Sit down, please,' the officer said. Then he paused for a deep breath, and continued to speak. I sat down. The officers sat down opposite me.

'We've been alerted to some very bad news for you,' he said, pausing again. 'We think that you're on an IRA hit list, and that the IRA intend to kill you.'

'What!' I exclaimed. 'Why would they do that?' I added coyly.

'*You* might be able to tell us that,' he said. 'But our informant is adamant that the IRA are preparing to kill you, and that they have been preparing the ground for such a killing.'

'Why but?' I asked.

'Well,' the officer said, pausing again for a deep breath, 'there's rumours going about that you beat up a commander in their organisation. Is that true?' He looked me up and down, adding: 'you're a big man.'

'No,' I said. 'Who am I supposed to have beaten up?'

'You would know if you did it,' the other officer interjected. 'Have you been in a fight with anyone?'

'No,' I replied.

'Then maybe there's no good reason,' the first officer said. 'They do a lot of that.'

'How could this be true?' I asked. 'They would need a reason.'

'We think you know the reason,' the other officer interjected. I noted that they didn't tell me their names, as was common procedure among RUC personnel, who would be wary that the information might fall into the hands of terrorists.

'Well,' I said shrewdly, 'I can't think of any.' The two men looked at each other, with a certain amount of distaste for me, which I could sense, and a certain amount of confusion as to what to do.

The senior officer continued: 'We thought it would just be a formality this morning. I mean you should just get on the next boat to Britain, and flee this city. You're not safe here.'

'I'm not going anywhere,' I said firmly. 'I can check with the SDLP in the city, and they might be able to tell me exactly what the threat is.'

'Of course you may,' the senior officer said in his legalistic monotone. 'But we're pretty sure that you've been seen having troubles with the republicans, and that a senior republican was admitted to Altnagelvin Hospital with wounds consistent with a bad beating. You might not have done it, but you're getting the blame.'

'We can't offer you security,' the junior officer added. 'Well, we can help you to get to the ferry, and put you in touch with a few organisations who will help you, but we can't give you priority security.'

'I don't want your protection,' I said. 'I've nothing to fear from those people. It must be some misunderstanding.'

The senior officer rose to his feet, and the junior officer did likewise a few seconds later, and they smiled at me nervously, as if they realised that I was no friend of theirs.

'We've passed on our warning, sir,' the senior officer said, 'and offered our help. Here's my card if you want to tell us more, or if you want our help. We can do no more for now.'

'You be very careful,' the junior officer said. 'Our informant is usually very reliable.' Then they departed.

They didn't even mention the file, even though police officers were aware that it had gone missing. But that was typical of the RUC: the ordinary police and the Special Branch were to all intents and purposes separate organisations, and what one knew the other might very well not know.

But at least I was sure that there was a threat now. All the nervous energy and the irritating twitches I had become accustomed to over the previous few days were validated. I was going to be shot.

I was not a happy camper. The first thing I did was to ring a political friend of my father in the SDLP. He was confused about what I was saying, but he took it seriously nonetheless, and told me that he would do some checks.

He came back to me later that morning with the message that there were republicans who believed that I had "a case to answer" in relation to the beating of a republican in the city. But he said that he had told them to back off, and they were thinking about it.

'Did they mention a file?' I wondered.

'No,' the SDLP man said. 'They mentioned a beating Danny Murray got.'

I smiled at the thought of Danny taking a beating on my behalf, in order to cover for the real purpose of the threat to my life. It couldn't have happened to a nicer man. The SDLP man continued: 'Apparently he's on a life support machine.'

'That's terrible,' I said. 'But I didn't go near him.'

If Danny was that seriously beaten, then they intended to kill him, I thought. He had possibly done something to offend them. Perhaps he had botched his mission to deal with me. But, no, it seemed much more serious than that, and they had possibly used me as an excuse to get rid of him.

I rang a few people to see what I could find out. Only one, Brian, a close friend, was willing to talk to me about the matter.

'Danny got what he deserved,' he said. 'He's a bad bastard. He's been up to a lot of things, feathering his nest at the expense of the republican movement. They take a dim view of that.'

'They're trying to say that I did it,' I said.

'Good on you if you did, I say,' Brian stated merrily. 'But I don't think you're capable of doing that to someone.'

'Have you heard the rumours?' I asked.

'Oh, yeah,' he said. 'There are always rumours. I'll just wait to see who gets the bullet.'

His words sent a chill up my spine. He was right. There were always rumours when something like this happened. And it was always the case that people believed that whoever was punished, by getting "the bullet", was responsible. He had been held to be guilty in the kangaroo courts of the republican movement.

The IRA were engaged in a serious vendetta against me. They were setting me up for the fall, or "the bullet" as Brian had said. I was nervous. It suddenly hit me that I was really nervous.

I should have realised that they wouldn't take a rational view of our dispute. There had been no anonymous phone calls, or bricks through my window, over the previous few days. They were treating my case on an altogether more serious level. I had humiliated them and they wanted a result. The only result was to be my death.

I had to get out of my apartment. I was suffocating in there, alone and ready to die at any moment. I wanted to be sure that I didn't die there, like a rabbit trapped in a hole. I got into my car and drove, not really knowing where I would go. I wanted to ensure that I had thought through all my options.

There was no going back now. I had made my stand, and the Provos didn't like it. I had stood up for the only dignified approach to resolving my part in the work on big Tom Brennan's file. I had retained his file, and made them get someone else to do their dirty work.

I was not one of their soldiers and they were not carrying out a war in my name. They were not carrying out a war in the name of the Ireland that I believed in. They were rejecting the central thesis of the Irish nation, that we go everywhere in the world and make friends, not enemies.

They were making enemies for the Irish people and redefining what it meant to be Irish. I would have no part in that. Their petty agenda was to destroy and wreck in order to gain an Irish unity that I believed could only come through the extension of friendship of Irish nationalists to Ulster unionists.

No wonder they couldn't rest when I had made my protest by retaining the file. It was the rational thing to do and yet they couldn't see that. Their whole organisational goal was irrational. They were an irrational organisation that fed on the gospel of revenge. They always had to score even. That was in their nature.

What they were doing in the North was scoring even for fifty years of misrule by the unionists. They weren't interested in a just society. It meant nothing to them. If it did, they would have accepted that I had the right to protest at being used by their organisation.

They were interested only in carrying out vendettas, where more than likely they would be scoring even with people who had in reality done them no harm. They believed in the Old Testament dogma of "an eye for an eye and a tooth for a tooth".

Though sometimes it was more convenient for them to score even first. It was convenient in my case, and I resented that.

As I was driving outside Derry city in county Donegal, I decided to visit Doon Well again, to make my peace with God before I went to meet Him.

Chapter Twenty-two

I arrived at the shrine almost an hour later and went straight to the holy well. I drank a cup of the water of the well, which was said to have healing properties. I felt refreshed, as I had done on many occasions before. A few trickles of the freezing cold water went down my neck and under my shirt. I cringed on feeling its coldness.

I got up from the kneeling position beside the well, and went over to the bush. There, all the little mementos the sick people had left as a bribe to the spirit world to hear their prayers were dangling from the leafless bush. It was a tawdry sight, but when the leaves would grow back the mementos wouldn't be so noticeable, and the bush would serve its purpose as a place of prayer and devotion.

I decided to take my key ring off, not having anything else with me. I dangled it on a branch of the bush, which was just after its winter trim. I said my prayers then.

I prayed that God would protect me from the murderous IRA, and that I would be safe. I prayed that he would stop these murderous terror gangs that ruled sections of my home city. I prayed for forgiveness for the many sins I had committed.

I felt so relieved to have made my peace with God. I felt sure that the warning from Special Branch meant that an attack on me was imminent. I was sure that I was at serious risk of dying.

However, I wasn't going to take it lying down. I was going to do something, even if it would only be a final protest at being threatened with death. In my mind I knew what to do. It was clear that I had to do it. I had to make sure that the file got into the hands of the RUC.

That was the thing to do. It was the logical answer to their threats. They were going to kill me, and so I had to ensure that their organisation was embarrassed as much as possible.

The IRA had no right to fight on behalf of the Irish people. I didn't want them to fight on behalf of the Irish people. They were not fighting in my name, but in the name of an evil so perverse that it had to be Satan himself. They were evil, simply.

They were going to kill me for a start for my brave attempt to protest at their using of me for cover while they smuggled an IRA gangster through an Inland Revenue tax investigation. With their urgent desire to kill me, they were choosing a gangster over me, like the Jews had chosen Barabbas over Jesus.

I took another swig of the holy water and went back to my car. I drove straight back to Derry, without any stops on the way. Then I drove to my parents' home, and retrieved the file from my briefcase. I didn't want to give the police my briefcase in case they decided not to open it before handing it back to me.

Something told me that I had to be careful how the police came into possession of the file, so I thought about my options for a while. I drove to the city centre as I thought about what to do.

I considered leaving it in a solicitor's office, so that they would take it immediately to the police. But, no, the solicitors were dodgy. Danny Murray was one of them. There was a chance that they might be aware that the IRA was looking for a file.

As I came around a corner out of the professional district of the town, I saw a couple of tramps. They could do with the money, I said to myself. I stopped the car, and got out. I walked up to the tramps and said "hello".

'How would you like to make some money?' I asked innocently.

'We might do, mister,' one of them said. He was relatively sober-sounding.

'I'll give you twenty pounds if you take this file to the police station down the street,' I said.

'Forty pounds,' the second tramp interjected quickly with his increased demand.

'It's a deal,' I said.

'You'll find that there's a reward for £1,000,' I said cunningly. 'You should get the file down there straight away or someone else will get it.'

The two tramps split the two twenty pound notes that I gave them, and tottered off in the direction of the police station. I watched them the entire way from a distance. They entered the police station, and came out ten minutes later with big smiles on their faces.

They were hopping and skipping along as if their feet were as light as feathers. They seemed really happy, as if they had just secured a month's supply of drink. They would have to wait for the reward to be paid, but knowing that it was theirs when it came must have been the icing on the cake.

They practically leapt into the first public house they came past to spend the twenty pounds each that I had given them. They were floating on air and I was very tempted to go in and see what they were saying. But they might have jumped all over me and given the game away to the local punters.

The next part of my plan was to telephone Special Branch to ensure that they were aware of the file and its contents. I rang them straight away from a call box.

'A file has arrived in the possession of Strand Road RUC,' I told them. 'It contains the key to IRA business transactions on offshore islands.'

'Who are you?' they asked.

'That's not important,' I replied, my handkerchief over the mouthpiece to muzzle my voice.

'Thanks anyway,' the voice said. 'We'll deal with it immediately.'

'Don't thank me,' I said. 'Thank the tramps.'

'What?' he asked.

I put the phone down. I didn't want them thanking me. I hadn't done it to aid their cause. They were just as bad as the IRA in many ways, with their corrupt use of loyalist paramilitaries to attack and murder innocent Catholics. I had done it to secure my final act of defiance against IRA oppression of my community.

They were not going to dictate to me that I must remain silent in the face of an investigation that revealed that the IRA had in its possession millions of pounds in order to fund its campaign of terror, a campaign that they said was being carried out in my name.

I didn't want the Ireland that they would secure with their violence. It would have been founded on the blood of the innocent, on both sides of the political divide. I wanted an Ireland that lived up to its reputation as a land of saints and scholars. I wanted an Ireland that was free, not an Ireland that was beholden to gangsters and thugs.

Their thugs had practically murdered one of their own associates, Danny Murray, in order to set me up to be killed. That was perversion. It was profoundly evil. It didn't come any lower than that.

I went to the hospital next to see if Danny was still alive. I had to be careful not to be seen by any republican stragglers who might recognise me. I was careful, but as I entered the ward, there was a rush of nurses and doctors towards the Intensive Care Unit, and all eyes were on the door of the unit.

I stood there, not knowing what to do with myself. I wanted to walk back out while everyone was watching the door, but I couldn't. A nurse emerged after five minutes.

'I'm sorry,' she said. 'Mr Murray has just passed away.'

'Fuck,' a man in front of me shouted. 'I'll kill that bastard with my bare hands.' He banged his fist off the wall as if he meant business, but then broke down in tears. 'He was my wee brother,' he cried, as the nurse comforted him.

"That bastard" was me. I knew it and I made my way to the exit door. They were blaming me. As usual, the republican families swallowed everything that the IRA said.

There was a supreme irony in the fact that the man who had hounded me the most, and who had caused me the most grief, was lying dead in a hospital bed intended for me. I should have been dead, not him.

Perhaps it was the last nail in my coffin that they had got the death that they needed in order to justify their attack on me. They would now be free to trade that death for mine. I was a dead man. I knew it and they knew it.

The missing file would secure that when Special Branch made their moves. The IRA would go ballistic.

Nevertheless, the fact was that they intended to kill me anyway, and I had just got even with them "before the event", as they would say with their perverse logic. It was the least I could do in the circumstances.

I ate out in a Chinese restaurant that evening. I wanted to have people around me so that I could experience a final burst of the warmth of human company before I went to my death.

I felt a strange affinity with Jesus as I sat there. Perhaps it was the wine I was drinking having an effect. But I felt very close to the saviour. He had saved the world by conquering death as I had saved some lives by my desire to stand up to the IRA.

I had conquered death in a sense in that I was no longer afraid to die. I was sure that I was going to die. I could run away, but the IRA would find me. I wasn't going to live anonymously in some distant part of the globe. They would find me if I didn't try to live anonymously.

Strangely, I didn't mind dying. It was living like some republican rent boy or stooge that worried me. That's the way I would have had to live if I gave into them and their bribes. I would be one of them, just as guilty of their murders as if I had pulled the trigger myself. I felt good about my protest in that sense.

I had stood up to the IRA and I had conquered them and their evil ways. They would kill less people from now on in. I was sure of that. They would be damaged.

That night I slept better than I had done for weeks. I was content in the knowledge that I had followed my conscience, and refused to be intimidated or bribed by this evil organisation that called itself the Irish Republican Army. They were a bunch of cowards, murderers and thugs so far as I was concerned.

I hoped they would kill me in my sleep when they did it. It would be the final statement of their cowardice that they would sneak up on someone asleep. I expected to waken up in heaven.

But I didn't. The best laid plans of mice and men and all that. I woke up scared. I was tense, nervous, and very fearful of leaving my apartment. It was to be several days before I found out whether or not I had a future.

Epilogue
Thirteen years later

All that happened thirteen years ago. I didn't die, as one might have guessed, though I had an extremely tense few days after that fateful day when I decided to give the file to Special Branch.

I went back to work the following Monday after assurances that the file would be returned to our firm as soon as practicable. The Special Branch of the RUC were not going to hold onto it, they told us.

I can only guess as to why they wouldn't have considered it hot material. Perhaps they were too stupid to realise the extent of the information they had on big Tom Brennan. Perhaps they were not financially literate enough to realise that they had a proven case on their hands of a terrorist godfather.

But most likely, as this is Northern Ireland, and not a rational country, they decided to use the file to lever concessions out of the IRA, rather than as evidence that a man was holding funds to enable a terrorist organisation to conspire to maim and kill people in pursuit of a goal that simply could not be achieved down that route.

The reality was that it was possibly a case of the senior members of the two warring factions, as with all warring factions, getting off with blue murder. The big boys always got off, and the canon fodder at the bottom died or went to jail.

Big Tom Brennan lost most of the illicit money in any case, the Inland Revenue ensuring that he was stripped of any spare cash that might have made it look like crime pays.

The biggest surprise for me was a telephone call a few days after the file was handed over to the police from that same prominent businessman who had offered me ten thousand pounds for the file.

He gave me this complaining, as well as tension-lifting, story of how some people were trapped in "this situation" and of how they would "very dearly like to get out of it". I presumed he meant the IRA campaign, and I assumed he meant that there was no longer any animosity between them and me.

I could never really understand why. I can only assume that I had helped them in some small way out of the mess they had got themselves in, and they had somehow decided to pull the curtain down on the IRA campaign. Perhaps Special Branch had screwed a deal out of them that meant they had to stop the killing, and part of that deal meant that I was a safe man.

It made sense that if they attempted to kill me it would bring more publicity for the file, and for big Tom Brennan, who must have been sweating bullets after Special Branch got hold of his file.

I never really understood what happened to make me safe, but the violence mostly stopped in August 1994 with the IRA ceasefire, and there is relative peace now in 2004 A.D., and I feel safe.

A few weeks after I had visited Doon Well, I returned to the shrine and collected my key ring with gratitude. It was mission accomplished. The fairies had been kind to me. They realised that I didn't want to die.

A few months after I left her on the island, Carole-Anne rang me at work to tell me that Brigid and Kieran had split up but that she was getting married again soon to her long-time boyfriend in Dublin, after her mother had sadly passed away. I was a guest at the wedding, though a guest with a secret.

I took Bernie to the wedding in order to confirm to her "friends" that she had not blown her cover. We split up again straight afterwards, and it was ages before I met anyone I really liked.

When I did meet someone special, my beloved Patricia, we got married in October 1995, and have two lovely children,

Mary Carole and Patrick Bernard.

  I am a happy man now and my conscience is still clear. I continue to hold the view that it is better to live for Ireland than to die for her.